M000166417

VERMIN SUPREME

PRESENTS

2001 ©SETH

i PONY

Blueprint For a New America

bobtimystic
BOOKS

I Pony: Blueprint For a New America is another Bobtimystic Books project.

Copyright © 2016 by Vermin Supreme

Design & editing:
Bob Makela

Art by: Vermin's artist friends

ISBN-13: 978-0-9978520-0-4

Manufactured in the United States of America
First Edition
Second Printing

To order this book or to contact the publisher go to:

www.BobtimysticBooks.com

Suggested retail price: $13.00

For Becky.

"If you want a picture of the future, imagine a rubber boot on a human head—forever." *

~George Orwell

* Or something like that.

prologue #1

"Daddy, Daddy, Daddy!"

"Before we go to bed, will you tell us the story of how it was in the olden days, when Grandpa was a little boy."

"Sure, honey. That was before I was born, but I know a little bit about it. Once upon a time... before the new world where we live today came into being, there was a time when people could drive a machine powered by motors fueled by a magic liquid called gasoline."

"Gasoleeen?"

"There was a time when fossilfuelmen used giant drill machines to penetrate the crust of the Earth and dig...deep...down into the bowels of the planet."

"Ewww. Grossssssss," Asher said scrunching up his face.

"Like a well digger!!!" squealed Charon.

"Exactly, but these men were not digging for water. They where drilling...for oil! "

"But oil comes from whales!" said Asher, his face suddenly serious.

"Well, yes, child, today it does. Back then there were no giant whale farms."

"Well, what was there?"

"I'm trying to tell you. Patience, little ones," he said with a chuckle.

* * *

It was amazing no one had thought of it sooner. After all of the fish in all of the seven seas had been caught and eaten, the whales were the only things left.

Other than a few backwards nations, almost nobody wanted to eat them. They tasted terrible.

It was these backwards whale-eating countries that pioneered modern day industrial whale farming. They were motivated and hungry. Not in the motivated innovator-slash-inventor sense. Just hungry.

It was, naturally, the Americans who realized whales could be used for lubricating oil once again. All those whales. All that unused lubricating oil swimming around. It just made sense. Otherwise the oceans were simply going to waste.

There was nothing in the International Whaling Bans against whale farming. That's for sure.

* * *

"Back then, the olden day people pumped

up oil from under the ground," he continued.

"There were whales under the ground?"

"No, of course not. There were pools of oil under the Earth's crust."

"Swimming pools?"

"Bread crusts?"

"Whales in swimming pools?"

"...with bread crusts?"

The twins were clearly enjoying themselves. Nonplussed, he answered their playful queries.

"More like underground oceans of oil, without the whales. And, yes, the crust of the Earth is, indeed, like the crust on a loaf of bread."

Looking around the room, he hoped for some play object that he could use as a model. The colorful and lovingly reconditioned ancient plastic toys, pulled from some faraway archeological landfill and transported by land, gave him a warm sense of nostalgia for a past he had never personally experienced.

He opted instead for the jumbo sketchpad and a box of crayons.

"Now this is the Earth's crust. It is the top layer on the surface—where we live."

He drew a brown scribble line for dirt and a green scribble line on top of that for grass. Then he drew a little house and a tree.

"Underneath the crust was oil." He indicated the oil with a black crayon scribble.

"Underneath the oil, there's rock," which he illustrated with irregular, gray crayon circle shapes.

Unleashing his creativity, he went for broke.

He furiously drew a red, orange and yellow orb to represent the molten rock magna in the center of the Earth.

"Underneath the rocks, lava."

"Lava! That's where volcanoes come from," offered Charon excitedly.

"Close enough," he smiled. "And once they pumped up the oil, they changed the oil into gasoline."

"How?" the twins demanded in unison.

"Science!" He thundered the word in a loud, dramatic dad voice.

* * *

He got on with the story.

"Once upon a time, there were great cities far to the east and far to the west. They say they were grander than New Detroit."

"Grander than New Detroit?"

"Yessssss. Millions of Americans lived in those cities and rode across the land in the gasoline carmachines. One day, finally, the oil ran out and the great herds of carmachines were no more.

"People were very sad.

"After the oil was all pumped out by the fossilfuelmen with their pumping machines, there was great friction between the layers of the Earth."

He gesticulated at his crude drawing. "There were great earthquakes. The great cities crashed into the sea."

In explaining, he was simultaneously paraphrasing the worst catastrophe to ever hit the continent—while glossing over the utter devastation and human suffering of the unprecedented event.

To illustrate the devastation, he shook the jumbo drawing pad vigorously and dropped it to the straw-covered dirt floor. The burst of air blew dust and bits of straw into the air.

"Yes, they did," he said somewhat softer.

After the dust settled, he continued.

"Your great-grandfather"—he raised his left hand—"who lived in the west"—then stretched out his left arm—"and your great-grandmother"—he raised his right hand—"who lived in the east"—then stretched out his right arm—"met in the middle."

His thumb pinched up against his fingers. He made his hands bounce towards each other until they touched, then made a kissing noise.

"Ewwww," said the twins simultaneously.

"That's right, kids. If it weren't for all the oil running out, the giant earthquake, the mass destruction and the great migration—they never would have met in the refugee camps. My mother would never have been born. I would never have been born. And you never would've been born.

"But here we are. Right here in the future. The end."

* * *

"Today all our energy needs come from renewable resources," he said, taking pride in his canned, pro-industry talking points.

"Daddy, will you tell us about the electricity factory where you work?" requested Asher Lee.

"How do magnets work?" chimed in Charon.

"Some other night, pumpkins."

He had no idea how magnets worked.

He did know, however, that the story of electricity in America was literally the stuff of nightmares.

"Now get to sleep." He kissed them both on the forehead.

Then he tossed some broken bits of furniture and a few hardcover books into the cast iron stove that would keep them warm until morning.

prologue #2

Chuck's eyelids leapt open as his nose choked on the sharp acrid smell of burning plastic.

Knowing immediate danger when he smelled it, and sensory overload when he experienced it, he tried to get a grip on the rapidly rising panic that his lizard brain was inducing.

He looked around wildly through the chaos trying to assess the situation. Alarms and warning sirens filled his ears. Instrument panels sparked and sputtered. The smoke and the blinking danger lights gave the cramped space the look of a hellish disco.

Through the porthole, a calm beam of sunshine pierced the smoke and darkness. His eyes landed on the beam. He was able to orient himself in the cabin.

The steady voice of the ship's computer calmly made its pronouncement.

"Please evacuate the capsule..."

He quickly came to the conclusion that his time and spaceship, *Continuum*, must have crash-landed on some unknown planet.

"Well that's a fine kick in the ass," he said to himself as he realized that he was up to his shins in water.

The ship was sinking rapidly.

* * *

Each and every one of the inflatable flotation gizmos—which were specifically designed to keep the stupid spacecraft afloat in just such an event— had obviously failed to deploy. The computer made a most welcome announcement.

"Atmosphere capable of supporting life..."

His rigorous training kicked in as he un-strapped his safety restraints and reached for the lever that would blow open the capsule door.

BOOM!

The door blew open, arcing through the air and landing with a splash. Sunlight and fresh air— and fresh water—flooded the cabin.

It was a beautiful day.

Filling his lungs with fresh air, he was able to regain his composure and reassess the situation.

Looking about the rest of the capsule, it was clear his fellow krononauts had not survived the trip. He winced at the sight of his desiccated colleagues. Then the perky synthesized voice chip chirped.

*"Self-Destruct sequence activated.
Three minutes until vaporization."*

Something had tripped the self-destruct mechanism. Believing that three minutes was plenty of time, Chuck quickly grabbed his kitbag, his seat cushion—which also acted as a flotation device—and his inflatable life vest.

His spaceman ray gun, much to his chagrin, was secure in the gun locker right in front of his face.

"Two minutes until vaporization."

There was not going to be enough time to enter the required information into the required fields to unlock his weapon. He could see it, but he couldn't get to it.

"Damn waiting times!"

He punched at the plastic glass that stood in his way.

"Fuck," he swore. He really wanted his gun.

* * *

Chuck waded over to the hatch and stepped up on its lip. Water poured up and over his time shoes and into the capsule. He looked down.

"Dammit! My favorite time shoes." They were, indeed, some really nice time shoes.

He blinked and squinted into the bright sunlight. He felt its warmth on his stubbled cheeks.

Chuck shielded his eyes from the sun and scanned the horizon, noting the direction of land.

Pausing momentarily, he said something somber and witty about his deceased coworkers in regards to their imminent burial at sea. Something about the captain going down with the ship.

"Goodbye, my Captain," he saluted.

* * *

Lest he be sucked into the undertow from the sinking ship, or caught up in the vaporization, Chuck jumped clear. In an instant, he was furiously swimming and kicking away.

"One minute until vaporization."

Bolts of electricity crackled around the skin of the sinking capsule. As the space machine submerged, the water sizzled and boiled as steam bellowed skyward. The computer voice burbled as it went under.

"30...blub...blub...seconds...glug...'til..."

Exactly 29 seconds later, the ship imploded.

As the machine destroyed itself, it produced an awesome shockwave that rolled over the water's surface. The three-foot swell lifted him up and set him down. It did not propel him forward in the least.

He paddled and kicked, kicked and paddled, until he could paddle and kick no more. He made it to the beach, pulled himself up onto land. Sucking hard for air, he blacked out.

There was no turning back.

*   *   *

Before Chuck opened his eyes he could half remember his dream. A smile crept across his face. He felt the warmth of the day on his closed eyelids. A slight breeze caressed his skin.

He was unsure as to where he was. Was he still in deep suspension on the ship?

He did know that if he was experiencing this level of consciousness, the ship was approaching its destination and bringing him online.

Slowly, he opened his eyes. He knew in a flash that he was no longer in space.

Looking about, he found himself surrounded by humanoids.

They looked like hippies.

They were hairy all over and seemed to have no shame. They seemed to be unable to speak coherently and they smelled terrible.

The ripe tribe eagerly welcomed the lost man into the fold.

*   *   *

Chuck had hoped these savages might treat him like a god. But it wasn't to be. Instead, they treated him with a kindness usually reserved for idiots or children.

He spent several days tagging along, joining them in eating nuts, berries, squirrels and other small mammals.

He was convinced one of their females was checking him out.

If this was going to be his new life, in this strange new world, he definitely wanted to get laid.

The tribe members' animal skin loincloths left little to the imagination. The women bared their breasts as if they were just another body part.

There were worse planets to be stranded on, he thought.

* * *

One fine day, as they made their way through the jungle, Chuck stopped to take a dump. The tribe continued down the trail. If nothing else, this new diet was keeping him regular.

Chuck was on his haunches defecating several feet off the path when there appeared to be a hubbub at the front of the foraging expedition. He was cursing the lack of toilet paper on this otherwise serviceable planet when he noticed the commotion.

He finished wiping his ass with some leaves, which he hoped were not poisonous.

No sooner had he pulled up his krononaut britches when he heard what sounded like a stampede. Several of the hippies ran back past Chuck in the direction from which they had come. The tribe personified fear as they scampered by, being chased by who knows what.

Within seconds, Chuck had been scooped up in a net and was being dragged along the ground.

After a short, but bruising, drag along the jungle floor, he found himself being released from the net.

Chuck and his fellow captives were surrounded by fierce, smallish horses snorting through their nostrils and kicking up dirt.

* * *

Attracted by his strange tattered astronaut garb, two members of the hunting party came up to Chuck. They reached out to touch the odd fabric.

Chuck snarled loud and clear. "Get your dirty hooves off me, you stinking ponies!!!"

The ponies in the hunting party were stunned. Never before had they heard a human talk, let alone accuse them of smelling.

With their superior pony strength and numbers, the pony soldiers quickly subdued the struggling man. They attached a massive yoke around his shoulders.

Chuck was chained to the other human captives and led down the trail towards New Pony City.

* * *

Marching him through the jungle, the ponies taunted him.

"Do it again, say something," they challenged Chuck as they poked him with sticks.

"You smell!" said another, fanning the air with a hoof.

Chuck decided to shut the fuck up and uttered not another word.

Shackled and naked in the lab, he listened as the pony scientists, wearing pony lab coats, went about discussing his imminent vivisection.

"We must cut him open and find out what makes him talk," said Dr. Zaius.

"I want his brain!"

"Let's cut off his balls!"

"Maybe we should keep him awhile and experiment on him alive before dissecting his brain," said Dr. Zira, a lone voice of pony reason. "We could still cut his balls off."

"We will discuss this tomorrow," said Dr. Zaius, who was famous for putting off important workplace discussions until the next day.

They all left the lab and headed home to their stalls and paddocks.

*   *   *

That evening Dr. Zira came back to the lab to check in on the human prisoner. She glanced at Chuck through the bars with a gaze both tender and curious. She'd never looked at a human in such a way before.

With apprehension and trans-species lust aroused, Dr. Zira approached the cage. They longingly looked into each other's eyes.

She stepped closer.

He reached out with his arm and stroked her muzzle.

She rubbed her muzzle on his arm.

Trembling, her pony muzzle lips, pink and moist, moved towards the man's stubbled manmuzzle as his moved towards hers. They mashed their faces together between the bars. Their inter-species tongues intertwined.

Chuck almost gagged on his pony love's huge wet pony tongue. He felt her equine teeth on his cheeks.

He had his whole face in her mouth—and he was loving it.

Pony saliva poured down his neck. His nipples hardened. His fingers became enmeshed in her silky mane. He tightly hugged her muscular neck and pulled her towards him through the bars.

* * *

It was at this moment that Chuck burst awake from his dream.

His heart was beating heavily and he was soaked in sweat. He had a huge erection that he had been rubbing on Jane, his wife.

Jane, already nudged awake by his magnificent manhood, took a firm and steady grip of his studly saddle horn and positioned herself all reverse cowgirl style on it.

Not caring whether it was a piss hard-on or not, she rode it for all it was worth.

"Married people with kids should always get

it when they can," she reminded herself. As the sun's rays entered the room—joined at the junk like that, sliding up and down on the old disco stick—Jane really loved her life and her husband.

She went through her mental to-do checklist for the day as she approached her first orgasm.

Her eyes rolled back in her head.

* * *

Meanwhile, breathing heavily, Chuck could not let go of the image of Dr. Zira's big anime eyes and long pony eyelashes. The sexy pony lipstick, her sexy pony lips and that lab coat all remained vivid in his mind.

He wrapped his fingers in his wife's long hair, pretending that it was his dream lover's silky mane. He imagined what it might be like, being belly-to-belly making love with a pony.

He had spent a lot of time trying to visualize the mechanics of how it might work.

He watched his wife's ass bouncing up and down as he envisioned he was fucking a hot, hot pony pussy.

chapter 1

The worst of times were all but a fuzzy wuzzy, gauzy wawzzy, faraway memory.

It was almost as if they had never existed.

It was as if a bureaucrat had stuffed them into some office memory hole shredder in order to make confetti for some ticker tape parade.

But these here times now—these were the best time. All thumbs up, number one. A triple plus. All the best times of all the best times, all rolled into one, and then some.

The mediocre of times? Well, they were so mediocre that they had made no memorable impression whatsoever.

There was much happiness and merriment among the citizenry. A tsunami of contentment waterboarded over all the good faces of all the good peoples. It was, indeed, the bestest of ALL the times. LOL. A big 10-4, that is for sure, good buddies.

Nothing quite like it.

Totally and truly, the bestest of all the times.

Seriously, it was bitchin'. There were no doubts about it.

It was pretty much the most awesomest of times in all of history when you get right down to it.

Absolutely darn tootin', straight shootin', double plus good, baby.

Let me let you all in on a little secret, buck-aroos—it was. It was the best. I don't know why I gush, but I do.

There was absolutely no downside worth mentioning, none that this writer can possibly think of. It was truly, most definitely, the undisputed best of all the times.

Public opinion poll after public opinion poll agreed. Scientific survey after scientific survey confirmed it to be true. Common wisdom dictated.

Anybody who said otherwise was just itching for a fight.

* * *

The air was clean. Alfalfa grew everywhere. The chirping of songbirds filled the air. The sweet scent of pony pee tickled one's nostrils. Pony dust and dander danced in the sunbeams.

Fluttering butterflies frollicked with unicorns under rainbow skies. By unicorns, of course, it was meant ponies that had had a horn surgically implanted into their forehead. Lab unicorns were still a long way away.

The only known prototypes of lab unicorns had turned out to be frightening mutants.

The beautiful rainbows that crisscrossed the skies were just the latest and most colorful blend of incredible chemtrail technology. Geo-engineering had never been so wonderfully prismatic.

Just gorgeous.

The butterflies were not real butterflies, of course, butterflies having reached extinction long ago. No one alive today had ever seen a real one. These butterflies were little mini recon spy drones. They sure were pretty. They mimicked the living butterfly's movements of flight very well.

The sound of the songbirds was synthesized from speakers mounted in the artificial trees.

Needless to say, there were no songbirds.

* * *

War and famine had been eradicated, completely eradicated. Well, maybe not eradicated, exactly. Maybe not eradicated at all, I guess. When you get right down to it, redacted was more like it.

There was really just about as much war and famine as there was before, maybe more.

Industrial accidents still occurred with alarming frequency, along with violent crime.

At home and abroad, power plant meltdowns, workplace shootings, civil disorder, race riots, religious strife, terrorist attacks and such all took place just as often, if not more often, than ever.

Maybe sanitized would be a better word to describe the present state of affairs.

The important thing was that such unpleasant realities were simply unknown to the vast majority of the population.

There were no news channels anymore, that's for sure—another brilliant directive by the High Council of Internet Memes. Thank you, High Council of Internet Memes.

With no mass media constantly reminding people that everything was going to shit, they were more likely to focus on their immediate concerns.

They were less likely to be depressed, neurotic, nihilistic.

War and famine had been redacted, completely redacted, for a better world.

And although the promised weather domes were never completed, the 25-foot tall sections that were completed did act as a dandy wall to protect against invaders.

It also did a handy job of keeping the citizens in—for purposes of safety, of course. Otherwise, if you turned up missing, you might not be added to the safety statistics.

If you were not added to the safety statistics, it would be a very bad thing indeed.

* * *

Automobiles were a thing of the past.

Yes, one might occasionally see a horseless carriage from time to time. It was best to give any such vehicle wide berth. It was either a paramilitary dental militia or an insane warlord. Or both.

There was certainly one thing that all could

agree made these times so wonderful.

Vermin Supreme had finally become President of America.

* * *

It was a hell of a time for a zombie invasion.

But even if the people knew it was coming, would they care? I mean, that's why they voted for the guy with the plan.

Americans still had freedom of movement. Want to go somewhere? Just hook up your cart and go! Sure, it took a little longer. But there was no hurry anymore.

It was a simpler time. A new golden age.

After all, everyone had their ponies now. Ponies to love and care for. Ponies to talk to. Ponies to confide in.

Ponies as constant companions.

Gather around children and you shall hear...
a tale of life in the yesteryear.

chapter 2

Happy, mood-elevating chemicals—added to the nation's water supply through the use of multi-flavored, vitamin-fortified, flouride-enhanced fracking fluid—brought much joy to all who partook. Good attitudes and good teeth flourished across the land.

Family life was particularly euphoric.

"Honey! Don't forget your pony!"

"LOL. How could I forget my pony? I could just as easily forget I'm married to you!"

"Oh, Chuck!" she blushed.

"Kids, do you have your ponies ready for school?"

"Yes, Mom," they sang in unison.

"Did you clean your rooms...?"

They nodded.

"...and the stables?"

"Yes, Mom," said Asher Lee.

"Did everybody get their feed bag on properly?"

"Yes, Mom," said Charon.

This was a daily chore. Of course they had. No one wanted a hungry pony.

"Has every pony brushed their teeth?"

"Yesss, Mom." As if they weren't thoroughly indoctrinated and fully aware of the consequences of dental neglect.

"After school I want you to braid some ribbons into your pony's manes. Tomorrow is 'Ponyfication Day'!"

"Yeah!!! 'Ponyfication Day!' OK, Mom."

"All right, saddle up and get going. LOL," she said as she gave the children a playful swat on the behind.

* * *

The goal was laudable: to provide a pony to every single American citizen. To create a world in which every American—regardless of age, race, creed or income—was free to frolic and cuddle with their very own pony companion.

Yes, the transition to a full pony-based economy was not an easy one. There were some...grumblers...pony haters...in the beginning.

There were those that screamed "Big Government." These malcontents had been dealt with swiftly and harshly.

Many pundits argued that it would never work. They were sent to the work camps to be shown otherwise. They were impediments to the new utopia. Examples of the dangers of old thinking. Speed bumps in a world that had no use for speed

bumps any longer.

To create a new world omelet, you have got to break some eggs.

* * *

Everybody prospered under the new pony-based economy.

The field of Ponyomics became a required course for the bestest and the brightest. There was, of course, a Federal Pony Identification System. Citizens were required to possess their pony at all times.

One of the first acts of the new Vermin Supreme administration was the abolition of Congress. It was replaced with the High Council of Internet Memes as the legislative decision-making body.

Of course, this was a totally unconstitutional and stupid idea.

However, at that time in American history, dissent had all but disappeared. The Supreme Court had became a literal rubber stamp.

And the fact that all voting occurred on the Internet gave a whole lot of weight to the premise that individuals who had gone viral and become 'Internet famous' were best equipped to represent the citizenry, having received so many 'viral votes.'

They also worked cheap, much cheaper than the old Congress.

* * *

The Federal Reserve was quickly nationalized, with the High Council of Internet Memes seizing the reigns of monetary policy. It was just as quickly renamed the Federal Pony Reserve. If fiat currency was to be issued, it needed to be backed by something.

Ponies were the perfect medium of exchange.

But there were growing pains during the transition times. The Great Pony Bubble and the subsequent crash that almost completely ruined what was left of the American economy was a perfect case in point.

As Lord Supreme so accurately predicted:

"Once we have universal pony ownership, we will have equity in the ponies we own. Once we have universal pony equity, we will be able to borrow against it. Once we've established pony-based debt, we can create pony credit default swaps and triple-A bond markets and such. We are going to have a HUGE pony bubble in the economy. We all know that bubbles are great in the economy—while it's happening. THIS bubble, however, will be reinforced and steel belted and last forever."

Truly, a beautiful economic vision.

Sadly, the Federal Pony Reserve was not quite up to the task. But that was a long time ago. Before capital crimes became capitol crimes.

* * *

The children excused themselves from the table. They grabbed their electronic book bags as they headed out the front door to their waiting mounts.

As they rode under the apple tree in the front yard, Ash Lee picked four apples—one for him, one for his teacher and one for his pony.

And, of course, one for his teacher's pony.

They set out down the road, off on their way to school.

MARGEAUX A. HUFFINES-KEENER

chapter 3

There were harsh political realities when President For Life Vermin the First took office.

During the days of his ascent to the White House, there were over 300 million Americans living within America's previous borders.

At the time, there were only 200,000 ponies in the whole country.

It was a recipe for civil unrest.

And those were not just political realities. These were reality realities.

*   *   *

There was a very stark choice to make.

Would it be the mass execution of some 299,800,000+ Americans in order to achieve proper pony/human parity?

Or would the answer be something else?

It is certainly true that such a mass execution would create jobs. It would also lessen the country's dependence on foreign oil. It would be good for the environment.

But there were some clear drawbacks to consider. Mostly, they were merely questions of ethics and public relations.

During this time of widespread civil unrest, all options were on the table.

The Dental High Command was put on high alert. The Dental Re-Education Camps were readied. Homeland Dental Security coordinated with the nation's Dental Police Departments.

The militarization of America's Dental Police forces had been a great idea that was about to pay off. And not just in lower incidents of gum disease nationwide.

There were riots in the streets of numerous cities. And the Pulsating Water Pic Cannons knocked rioters off their feet and knocked the plaque right off their teeth.

*   *   *

The population was demanding their ponies. Ponies that were nowhere in sight.

It was a time of heightened international tensions. No one would have blamed Tyrant Supreme if he had ordered the National Dental Guard to carry out a full-scale massacre of the civilian population.

It was high time, actually.

The veneer of civility that had protected Americans from such real political unrest for quite some time was wearing thin. The quaint and oft repeated notion that "it can't happen here" was truly just a lack of imagination.

It didn't help at all that recently installed Dictator Forever Vermin Supreme was completely and utterly insane.

This was not evil old Richard M. Nixon's keep-the-Vietcong-on-their-toes-by-pretending-to-be-a-madman-strategy crazy.

This was not Ronald Reagan's early presidential onset Alzheimer's crazy.

No. Vermin Supreme was full-on batshit crazy. Delusional. Hallucinating.

The Commander in Chief was not only leaning towards using nuclear weapons. He was considering using nuclear weapons on American soil—against American civilians.

How this deranged hobo made it all the way into the White House was still not completely understood.

* * *

As the children rode down the street they encountered the first of several Dental Checkpoints.

"Smile, please," the inspector said, inserting his gloved finger into the pony's mouth and lifting its upper lip for a better gum inspection.

"Have you been flossssinggg? Whaaaat is your pony's name?"

"Butterscotch."

"And what is your name?"

"Asher Lee, sir."

"Have you been flossing Butterscotch's teeth?" he asked, pressing his face into the mouth of the animal to get a better look.

"Yesssss?" Asher said with uncertainty.

"Well her name may be Butterscotch, but her breath smells like shit."

* * *

Vermin's trusted Chief of Staff, Dr. Zakk Von Flash, eventually insisted he choose the thing-other-than-mass-murder as an option.

That thing-other-than-mass-murder option turned out to be a peaceful, Manhattan Project-style program for ponies. A vast operation whose goal was not an atomic weapon, but an atomic pony bomb of sorts—an atomic pony population bomb, if you will.

With a mandate of leaving no filly unbred, a full-tilt forced pony breeding system was put into action. A massive in vitro test tube pony program was launched.

Tens of thousands of horse and cow wombs now carried ponies.

There was a massive increase in funding for pony cloning—or clonies as they became known.

Possible conversion kits to bridge the pony gap were explored. By turning dogs and cats into temporary 'ponies' thru the use of prosthetics and various attachments, President Supreme, for a while at least, could claim to have solved the pony crisis.

The Pentagon had already been working on robotic ponies for quite some time. DAARPA had been bankrolling Boston Dynamics, a pioneer in robotic animal mimicry. Their four-legged all-terrain robot created quite a stir. Although nicknamed Big Dog, its motion was clearly equine, not canine. The possibilities of this equine-based quadriped as a military pack mule were soon obvious.

From there, it was a short trot to the mandatory civilian market. After Google bought up Boston Dynamics, the writing was on the wall. Yes, the early versions were somewhat terrifying. They certainly frightened children. This was a major problem in a universal rollout type of situation.

The high-pitched screaming whine of its engine was another one of its problems.

It was actually deafening.

When the developers brought the noise down to an acceptable level, there were sighs of relief all around.

The Department of Ponies had specified the robotic monstrosities be covered with soft, furry plush and be given big, super cute anime eyes. They seemed much less dangerous that way.

The best part of having Ponytopia on Earth come to pass in America was never, ever having to hear another child whine, "I want a ponyyyyyyyyyyyyyyy!!!!"

*   *   *

DARPA was also a major funder of Dr. Von Flash's Zombies for Peace and his peaceful zombie works.

The military application of zombies in warfare had been hotly debated. The use of zombies in warfare had been roundly condemned by the United Nations. Still, the U.S. reserved the right to use zombies in a 'defensive' capacity.

Zombies became a low-tech weapon of choice for terrorist groups. All it took was a rental truck full of zombies in a high density population center and...BAM!

There had been several zombie outbreaks on U.S. soil that were 'proven' to be terrorist attacks—when 'proven' simply meant a picture/word meme blaming some group had been released by the government.

When it was 'proven' that Oceana was responsible for one of these attacks, it was more than enough pretext to try out the new generation of Pony Drones—fearsome, flying, fire-breathing robots that could torch a wedding party like nobody's business.

There were eventually leaks that proved the CIA had used zombie infections against rebel soldiers in several outbreaks.

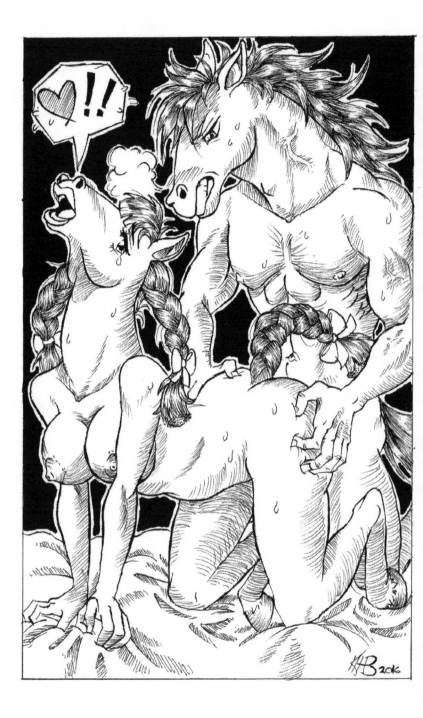

chapter 4

Using his scanner device, the man scanned the tattoo bar code on the pony's upper inner lip.

It was at this inopportune moment that Butterscotch decided to let loose with a round of flatulence of epic proportions.

The man and the boy both winced.

Charon let out a little titter.

Knowing full well that he could be fined for such an unauthorized methane release, Asher Lee gave his sister a very dirty look.

He dismounted his undersized steed. Not much of a dismount, really, seeing as how his feet almost touched the ground. This might be the last season that he could ride on Butterscotch's back.

Soon, he'd have to ride in a pony cart like the other biggers.

Asher unvelcroed his government issue pony pooper scooper. He expertly scooped up the road apples before they even had a chance to hit the ground, before fluidly flinging the poo into the checkpoint's pony poop collection target.

Given the national popularity of Ponyball, the hybrid sport combining polo and lacrosse, it was no surprise.

His deposit was dutifully recorded and the proper pony poop credits were added to his account.

Nothing was said between the two as the man, now using dental tools, continued the cursory dental exam on the pony's mouth.

* * *

The free pony program had served its purpose as a jobs creator. It created lots and lots of jobs. It was a job multiplier that had ripple effects throughout almost all sectors of the economy.

There was a surge in pony-related industries. Business was booming for saddle makers, alfalfa farmers and blacksmiths. The all but extinct buggy whip makers came back with a vengeance. The factories that produced American-made novelty pony hats and oversized pony sunglasses went into overdrive.

All buildings in America were required to be "Pony Accessible," providing thousands of jobs in all the trade industries. Detroit was retrofitted to produce pony carts and pony-based—and pony-friendly—mass transit systems. There were pony refueling stations. There were pony poop collection facilities.

There was virtually no unemployment, as every non-working American was conscripted into the Pony Poop Collection Corps of America.

Composting pony poop into fertile soil for America's future became one's patriotic duty.

* * *

"Dear, how is the Pony Poop Methane Digester running?"

"Great, Dear. We should have enough methane gas to heat our lovely home all winter."

"Wonderful."

"Chuck, we need to talk. I found this under Asher's mattress. I think he's been clopping."

"Well, that's normal for a boy his age."

"But look what he's been whacking to!"

Jane set down the porno viewer she had found under Asher Lee's mattress.

As Chuck flipped thru a few galleries, he was disturbed—but strangely aroused—by the cavalcade of images depicting fornicating anime anthropomorphic cartoon ponies. The come-hither look of half-human/half-pony hybrids was surprisingly seductive. He caught his mind drifting.

He cleared his throat and said, "I'll have word with the boy."

* * *

One thing about Internet memes—and by memes we mean macro images with words—is that many are not real and could not possibly participate in a deliberative body.

Keyboard Cat. Grumpy Cat. Trollface. Rage-face. Zoltar. They're all animals or cartoons.

Yet for every 10 unreal Internet cat memes, there was one flesh-and-blood human meme.

Even the human memes—Scumbag Steve, OverClingy Girlfriend, Bad Luck Brian—were not real. They were simply snapshots of individuals in a specific time that had led to ascribed meanings by others who added pithy phrases.

So it was the rare meme, a unicorn if you will, that was an actual person doing something as themselves that had gone viral.

Jimmy McMillan of The Rent Is Too Damn High Party was one such meme. Oklahoma apartment building fire evacuee Sweet Brown became a meme uttering—"Ain't nobody got time for that."

Vermin Supreme was another.

Alabama native Antoine Dodson became a meme when the news interviewed him after a bedroom intruder assaulted his sister. David after the Dentist became a meme while coming off dental drugs. "Is this real life?" indeed.

How these random Internet celebrities were supposed to come together as a functioning government body was still unclear.

* * *

Another agent approached Charon and began the familiar checklist.

"Smile, please."

Charon beamed her pearly whites as the agent waved the dental chip-reading wand in front of her front teeth.

"Pony's name?"

"Butterflyyyyyyyy."

"Purpose?"

"Me and my brother are going to school."

"What is your school?" she asked, knowing full well the answer.

"George Washington Bush Elementary."

The agent always enjoyed the way the people who named the school managed to pay homage to two great American presidents at once.

She scanned the pony's identification lip tat, admiring the sparkling pony choppers as she did.

"Nice pony teeth, kid. Now get going."

"But my brother..."

"I said GIT!!!"

Charon looked back to see her brother lying face down, spread eagle with his hands on the back of his head.

"Gee, mister, I didn't mean it..." she could hear him saying, as her pony mount was led to the other side of the chute and given a sharp swat to the ass. Butterfly broke into a gallop.

"Shit," Charon thought. "What now?"

chapter 5

After the last newspaper had folded, Internet memes were the only game in town.

The summation of all information and ideas crammed into single macro image photos, with words superimposed over them, became the predominate medium through which ideas were expressed. It simplified the issues considerably.

There had been a strange bastardization of American English into 'cat-' or 'dog-' speak in the official media. It was how most Americans got their information about the outside world around them.

It became known as 'memespeak.'

* * *

Meanwhile, back at the ranch...

Looking at the clock, Chuck knew he had plenty of time before he had to be at the office.

Quite frankly, in this new, reborn, rebranded, pony-based American economy, nobody really gave a damn if you were 'late' for 'work'—or early, for that matter.

Both words had been given new, elastic meanings that reflected the new reality on the ground.

As a matter of fact, you could miss entire days or weeks of 'work' without putting your job in jeopardy. There were more immediate things to take care of. Priorities had changed, radically.

The mandated victory gardens and livestock ownership changed the way America did things. The endless supply of nutrient-rich pony poop created bumper crops. The dependence on Big Agra and factory farms had diminished.

Monsanto had been nationalized and dissolved.

The dependence on transportation to move produce and livestock was reduced by over 9000%. Things had been decentralized on a very large scale.

When Americans stopped spending 15% of their income on groceries—thanks to everyone pitching in at home—people realized they could work even less.

* * *

It was just a playful little thing JR did.

Whenever he saw an alfalfa wagon, or any silage for that matter, he would point excitedly and shout—"Hay!!!!"

Asher thought this quite funny, every time.

His family did not.

This time it was even less funny.

Whatever humor the situation might have been worth was overridden by the fact of his current circumstances.

It was Asher's unexpected exclamation of the word "HAY!!!" at the checkpoint that startled the inspector, causing him to stab the sharp dental tool into Butterscotch's gums—causing Butterscotch to chomp down on the inspector's hand.

It was all Asher could do to stop himself from laughing at the sight of the red-faced, jumping, sputtering, hand-waving dental inspector.

The only thing missing was steam coming from his ears.

But this was not a cartoon. This was real life.

"Shut up," said the man as he jumped comically from foot to foot, shaking his hand wildly. "Your stupid pony bit me!"

"Fuck," thought Asher.

"I didn't mean anything by it, mister," he pleaded again.

His partner was wildly swinging his sidearm, pointing the gun alternately between Asher, then Butterscotch.

* * *

The First Council of Internet Memes Decree essentially ended landlordism as its first fully official act. Jimmy McMillan of The Rent Is Too Damn High Party was victorious, as he successfully argued against all and any rent. There was a proclamation across the kingdom declaring everyone the owner of their current domicile.

Boom. Just like that—no more rent. No more mortgages. No more need to work all those hours to pay the rent.

There was no rent. No car payments. You grew your own food. Heating and cooking fuel were readily convertible from pony poop. Secondary education was now free on the Internet.

And ponies. Free ponies.

It was shortly after that when the 25-hour work week was instated.

*   *   *

"I'll be stopping off at the blacksmith's shop today to pick up a new buggy whip," Chuck told his lovely bride.

"Oh, dear!" said Jane, her red lipsticked mouth making a perfect "O" as her eyes opened wide in mock surprise.

"I am going to smack your ass red tonight!!!"

"Oh, dearrrr!!!" she exclaimed, excited at the thought of the endorphin releasing sting of horse-hair on skin. "And then it's my turn!"

Chuck knew exactly what that meant.

"Mmmmmmm." He could feel his prostate twitch at the thought.

*   *   *

Chuck stood up and hugged his lovely bride, rubbing up against her. He kissed her deeply. They moaned together, their vocal chords vibrating in unison. She could feel his erection through his trousers.

She gave it a little rub.

He lifted up her skirt. She dropped her panties. He lifted her onto the counter in one smooth, practiced move. He entered her with the force of a wild pony stallion.

She began bucking like a wild bronco.

"Yee-haw!" she cried.

After it was over, he pulled up his trousers from around his ankles and buckled his belt.

He kissed her on the neck and picked up his briefcase.

"Give my regards to the alfalfa delivery man."

"Ha ha ha ha!!!"

chapter 6

At school, the class recited the mandatory Dental Hygiene Oath as delivered by Supreme Overlord Vermin Supreme during the Great Presidential Debate of 2011.

It was during this time that mandatory dental hygiene was really brought to the forefront of American presidential politics. Although it would take candidate Supreme 25 more years to get to the White House, it was these simple words that were adopted by a nation.

The story of his slow and steady ascent to the presidency, overcoming all obstacles—and his dedication to such a worthy cause—was an inspiration to the nation's youth. It was a story that had much more resonance than the George Washington chopping down the cherry tree meme. "He could not tell a lie!"

Utter bullshit.

* * *

Charon was distracted, as it became clear Asher Lee might miss roll call. The class had already begun to pledge their allegiance to victory.

"Gingivitis has been eroding the gum line of this great nation long enough. It must be stopped. For too long this country has been suffering a great moral and oral decay—in spirit and incisors. A country's future depends on its ability to bite back. We can no longer be a nation indentured. Our very salivation is at stake. Together we must brace ourselves as we cross over to the bridgework into the 23rd century. Let us bite the bullet and together make America a sea of shining smiles, from sea to shiny sea."

There is something mesmerizing about the sound produced by a classroom full of children repeating, in unison, the rote memorization of a string of words.

The sound of compliance.

The sound of commitment to unquestioned ideals.

The sound of consent.

Something akin to 5,000 zombies moaning "BRAINNNNNSSSnnnnn" all at once.

* * *

The teacher addressed the class.

"Today, class, we shall study chapter three in our history textbooks: 'The War on Narnia.' This

56

was America's first experience with interdimensional warfare. Once the portal was discovered in that wardrobe, the President decided that if we did not fight them there, in their world, we would have to fight them here, in our own world."

It was very similar to President Supreme's rationale for going back in time and fighting the Nazis in their own time, lest we fight them in ours.

Ever since time travel, portals and such became tools of foreign policy, Mr. Smith had to pay extra attention to his history textbooks. History could be radically altered by some careless or well-meaning krononaut messing with the space-time continuum. Mr. Smith had seen it happen once, mid-lesson. It was very disconcerting.

He'd heard a rumor that the Library of Congress had the means to collect all the alternative histories that had ever been written.

He'd sure like to take a gander at that!

* * *

"We'll start by reading the words of then-President Vermin's declaration of war," Mr. Smith began.

"As your President, I have promised to engage in hostilities only with those I deem to be a real and immediate danger to our peace-loving nation."

The children read the words as they appeared in the air, screened through the giant holographic head of Vermin Supreme slowly rotating.

"That is why I have ordered the Strategic Air

Command to begin the bombing of Narnia in five minutes. In this time of need, we must unite as a nation. I hope you will all pray for our terrible flying unmanned killer robots as they rain fire and death upon our subhuman enemy."

The hologram shook its giant fist at the air—as holographic, laser-shooting, flying roboponies flew around the giant head of America's first post-Constitution president.

Digital flames erupted around the classroom, perfectly timed with the surround sound explosions and the digital smoke. The *Themesong of America* welled up.

Learning American history had never been so much fun.

* * *

Asher Lee quietly tiptoed barefoot into the classroom, holding his shoes in his hands.

"Asher, how nice of you to join us. Tell me, what do you know of the American War for Narnian Independence?"

"I know they had it coming…Narnian bastards…" He completed the thought in his head.

He had never met a Narnian and couldn't find Narnia on a map. But, boy howdy, he sure did hate Narnians.

"…and I can tell you that they started it!"

The early propaganda news GIFs put forth by the Supreme administration, arguing for a Narnian invasion, were clearly video remixes of the classic movies from the early 2000s. The meme coverage of the war pretty much resembled a series of movie posters, in fact.

The movies were thereafter classified **Top Secret**.

A one-word headline that read 'WINNING" was enough information anybody really needed.

Media access to the battlefields was severely restricted. Occasionally, reporters were allowed into the magical wardrobe cabinet. For some reason, however, they were never able to pass through the portal and were left trapped in the locked piece of furniture. When the ranking officer was finally able to stifle his laughter, they were eventually released.

Doubters of the official narrative were flirting with treason. To question the narrative was to question reality itself. It would simply not do.

Old timers insisted it was fiction. They were begrudgingly tolerated.

Whether or not such a war had ever actually been fought was the territory of fringe conspiracy theorists.

chapter 7

Chuck made it past the last of the dental checkpoints and finally arrived at work. The full body/pony x-ray fast lane was definitely the way to go if you were in a hurry and didn't mind a few extra rotogens to the nads and noggin.

After parking his buggy, Chuck led his pony—Tony the Pony (federal pony ID no. 131-444-013)—to the employee stables.

He tipped Roy, the stable boy, a pony nickel.

There had never been an accidental zombie release in a commercially licensed Zombie Turbine Facility. The same could not be said about zombie storage or transport operations. These were technically not part of the Turbine Facility, thus did not sully their pristine statistics. Nor did it effect their ability to make the claim.

"Hello, Al," he said to the guard.

"Howdy, Chuck."

"Hello, Doris," he greeted the receptionist.

"Hello, Mr. Hesson."

He made his way to the locker room and removed his street clothes. Opponents used to jibe that more people had died in Vermin Supreme's car than in zombie plant accidents.

That was before more people got killed in zombie power accidents than in President Supreme's car.

* * *

Chuck suited up in his insulated, protective suit and entered the elevator that would take him down under the Earth's surface.

"Elevator going down. Next floor...Hell... Zombies...Ladies lingerie," he announced to no one.

Exiting the elevator, he walked to the door at the end of the hallway. He smiled broadly at the door, as the dental laser scanner scanned his teeth. It was confirming his identity, removing plaque and looking for cavities all at the same time.

The door opened.

The important thing to remember was that they were no longer human, Chuck reminded himself. As he headed down the metal stairs, his footsteps echoed through the stairwell. He pulled on his mittens and earmuffs. It was cold down there.

There had certainly been any number of human fatalities during the zombie energyfication program—a drop in the bucket compared to the Zombie Wars before it, to be sure.

Most of these deaths occurred during the early years of the program. Human error and stupidity were mainly to blame.

There were some zombie energy-related occupations that did have a higher danger rating than others. Freelance Zombie Wranglers had one of the more dangerous jobs, especially in the beginning.

Eventually, specialized zombie capture equipment came on line and minimized the risk.

Zombie Extraction Dentistry was also a hazardous human task before it, too, was automated.

Most surviving relatives were okay with giving consent for their zombie relatives—giving them a good home, if you will. It was an honest way for a zombie to make a living, or at least earn its keep. They got plenty of exercise, had plenty of company—and didn't kill people and eat their brains. For the comfort of all, many of the details of zombie energy harvesting were simply not discussed.

Inevitably, the zombie rights movement became a small, but vocal, force. However, they failed to gain much traction when the court, once and for all, agreed that zombies were, in fact, dead—and thus had no rights under the Constitution.

* * *

It was quite a sight to behold from his perch on the catwalk above the pit: a treadmill the size of a football field, with thousands of the undead moaning in unison—each in their own harness, slowly marching along.

The zombies themselves were practically perpetual motion machines, requiring almost no fuel. They could produce many kilowatts of electricity for practically nothing.

Clean, green and renewable, ZommPower was almost too cheap to meter. Almost.

The technological achievement of actually harnessing the awesome power of zombies had indeed proven formidable and taken several generations to perfect.

First of all was the problem of gear ratios and such. The early Hamster Wheel technology was laughably inefficient compared to today's standards. The real breakthrough came through the pioneering work of Dr. Zakk Von Flash. It was Dr. Von Flash who first was able to synch up formations of zombs using electricity.

It was when electrode implants became standard—allowing the zombs to be synchronized for efficiency—that large-scale zombie energy became feasible. Fabricating a zombie treadmill of such dimensions was truly an engineering marvel.

Zombie power produced zero emissions, other than the inevitable stench of rotting flesh. Dipping the zombies in polyurethane during their processing helped somewhat, but not much.

The ventilation systems in these energy facilities were very good, as was the overall working environment. There was a reverence and respect for the undead. They were the ones doing all the real heavy lifting. Cruelty towards the undead and necrophilia were strictly discouraged.

Photography was prohibited. The last thing the industry needed was some Abu Grahib-style photos being turned into news memes.

chapter 8

Chuck noticed a zomb in row 20, seat 5, had gone limp.

He reached down with his poking pole. Hoping to restart it, he gave the thing a couple sharp pokes from above.

His heart really wasn't into it, though. He was lost in his thoughts, which included some pony erotic daydreams.

Suddenly and without warning, the whole field of zombies malfunctioned en masse. Their relentless march forward ceased. Some sort of mass seizure was taking place. There was twitching, twitching everywhere...

Then they all stopped dead in their tracks and went completely limp.

But the monstrous treadmill, with all its inertia, continued in its direction for several hundred feet. The tethered, hanging zombies were dragged backwards by their toes and the tops of their feet.

The lights flickered as the treadmill slowly

ground to a halt.

*   *   *

There was a quiet that had never been heard since day one at the facilities operation.

It seemed like forever was hanging in the air, until a canned and calm female voice came over the intercom, intoning—

"Malfunction in sector G."

This seemed to wake the zombies up. The zombs reanimated en masse and regained their footing. Momentarily, they just stood there, swaying slightly. Then they began vocalizing.

Working at the Zombie Turbine Energy Facility for so long, Chuck thought he knew all the zombie noises—or 'songs' as they were sometimes known—but this one was new to him. It sounded electric.

It was as if they were all humming. Or maybe it was the beginning of an Om chant.

Either way, it increased in volume and frequency. From his vantage point on the catwalk, Chuck was completely stunned. He knew that he was witnessing and hearing something he might never see or hear again.

Then the small army of zombies did something very curious, indeed.

In unison, they began 'running' in small circles, as their tethers allowed counterclockwise. This turned into spinning, spinning counterclockwise as they picked up speed and centrifugal force.

They continued to pirouette, around and around, until the bolts that were holding them in place began to come unscrewed. One by one, washers and nuts hit the deck after becoming disengaged from the spindle. One by one the zombies hit the dance floor.

Splat...Splat...Splat...

Chuck's eyes grew wide.

Having very little balance, most found themselves in a heap or sprawled out all helter skelter. (Of course, 'found themselves' implies a self-consciousness, something zombs don't possess. It is always tempting to project human awareness and emotions on the undead automatons. Study after study has proven this to be untrue.)

Having little natural coordination, zombs generally had a very hard time getting themselves off the ground.

In the olden days, YouTube videos of zombies comically struggling like a beetle on their back—or propelling themselves in a circle on the ground like Curly from the Three Stooges—were quite popular. At the sight of so many zombs rolling and writhing on the ground, these wacky images flooded Chuck's memory. He began doubling over in laughter.

* * *

What happened next was unprecedented. The zombies went stiff and began to shudder. After another short seizure and momentary pause, the zombs—in a few efficient, if not completely graceful moves—lifted themselves off the floor.

Chuck stopped laughing and paid close attention. The hairs stood up on the back of his neck.

The horde of 5000 began to converge in one spot against the cement wall of the enclosure. If that spot was where the brain pile was, that would be perfectly normal.

But that was not where the brain pile was.

The zombies began to pile up on each other. They were hanging on to one another, crawling over one another, pulling themselves up on top of one another. Until...

They formed themselves into a giant inhuman zombie pyramid. The zombies on the bottom were being crushed to a pulp. Those in the middle of the heap were just crushed. This piling behavior enabled them to reach the top of the 15-foot wall, to the lip of their enclosure.

They finally climbed over the railing and spilled up onto the mezzanine and quickly filled the overlook, leaving behind dozens of squished, wriggling zombies slithering below on the treadmill.

Cooperation on this scale amongst zombies was simply undocumented. Zombies really didn't cooperate on any scale. Until now.

Something was truly amiss.

The fact that this was currently happening nationwide was a fact still unknown.

* * *

Chuck was feeling a little less safe up on his catwalk. He began to wonder if this wasn't some zombie version of the rapture.

Never before had hackers successfully breached a zombie turbine facility. There was a first time for everything.

All the nations' zombie energy turbine facilities were identical in blueprint. This was instituted as a cost-saving measure by the High Council of Internet Memes. It also made things exceedingly easy for just such a well-coordinated attack on the nation's energy infrastructure.

The zombies knew exactly which way to go to make good on their escape. They instinctively knew which door, which hallway, which turn to take. The doors were only secured against those trying to get in from the outside. There were no plans for this type of contingency.

The zombies emerged into the daylight for the first time in years. Their barely functioning eyeballs flooded with stimuli.

After emerging from the bowels of their enslavement, they reorganized themselves into formation and began to beat their chests. Dust flew everywhere,

Then, in unison, they let out a mighty, unholy inhuman roar.

The only humans outside that day were a few dozen plant workers. They were breaking for an extended lunch, playing cards, having a cigarette or maybe taking a dip in the employee hot tub. The plant pretty much ran itself. There was plenty of time for goofing off.

But when they heard that thunderous roar, every last living human jumped to their feet.

* * *

The lightly-armed security guards were the first to flee.

Once the zombie energy turbine facility staff realized that their worst nightmares were about to come true, much screaming and panicking ensued.

The legion of zombies turned the corner and entered the plant's plaza. The humans ran as fast as they could toward the glass doors of the atrium lobby. When they got to the doors, with the zombies closing in, they where horrified to find that they had been locked out.

In the event of an emergency, employees were supposed to meet up in the plaza and await further instructions.

At that moment, the only further instructions on their way appeared to be—How to Get Eaten By Zombies.

The people on the outside were in a frenzy, banging on the glass, begging to be saved. The people on the inside were shrugging, fidgeting, looking away—desperate not make eye contact with their doomed coworkers.

The zombie legion, in another miraculous first for the day, marched right past the humans. They didn't exactly ignore them, though. As the zombie column passed, not five feet from the humans, their heads would turn. Their nostrils would flare. They'd snarl, gnash their teeth and salivate.

If they could, they would. That was their unmistakable message.

* * *

After passing the cluster of relieved and uneaten humans, the zombies continued marching.

With the zombies gone, the glass doors of the atrium were unlocked. Those formerly on the outside of the locked doors streamed into the lobby. Tense arguments broke out as those who were almost eaten confronted their cowardly coworkers who were going to let the zombie feast go down. Several fistfights broke out.

Meanwhile, the zombies continued marching towards the employee stables. The stable hands fled in terror. Employees watching from the upper windows of the plant were horrified.

Then the zombies entered the structure.

Almost at once, the bickering and arguing ceased as the receptionist began screaming.

"Oh my God—the ponies!"

Stable became slaughterhouse, as 5,000 zombies worked their way through the building, one end to the other. The hungry zombie hoard made short work of the terrified ponies.

Being tethered to posts and trapped in stalls, the ponies didn't stand a chance.

* * *

The zombies, having gorged themselves during their first proper meal in a decade, became re-energized. They left the de facto abattoir and made their way towards the freeway. This scene was being repeated in dozens of cities and towns across what was left of America.

After the zombies had left the premises, everyone ran outside and towards the stables. They were met by a scene of bloody carnage. Oh, the horror...the humanity.

The employees lost it. They were inconsolable. One and all became a blubbering mess.

Blood and pony bones were scattered everywhere. There were no guts left behind.

Chuck, having emerged from the building into this scene, climbed on top of a picnic table and shook his fist in the air.

"Damn you, zombies!!! You'll pay for this!!! Nobody eats my pony!!!"

"Or," he added, "my children!!!"

As he said this, a touch of panic seized Chuck as he realized the zombie hoard was marching in the direction of the children's school...and his family's home. He jumped into action.

Knowing he was in desperate need of alternative transportation, Chuck left the grieving plant workers and ran to the motorstable.

He entered and approached the few mechanical conveyances still maintained in this day and age. Chuck looked around at the small collection of non-pony-powered vehicles. In the corner was a new-fashioned/old-fashioned steam-powered steamroller.

A smile crept across his face at the vision of himself high in the seat, rolling that monster through a horde of zombs, crushing them into dust. The satisfying popping sound of crushed skulls repeated in his head. "Take that!" his imaginary self shouted.

"Too slow," he thought. His eyes fell on the next vehicle—the company snow plow.

"Perfect," he said with a nod. Much faster, and with a plow blade that could plow through a blizzard of zombies. It would do nicely.

"Damn!" he exclaimed as he climbed into the seat. The snowplow was electric and hadn't been charged since last winter. The thing would take hours to charge. And besides, the zombies had 'pulled the plug,' so to speak.

* * *

Chuck went to the remaining vehicle.

He pushed the buttons and turned the knobs. He lit the pilot light that would start the powerful machine. It didn't start up right away though. These things took time.

First, the boiler would have to be brought up to heat. Pony methane provided the fuel that boiled the water.

Five...10...15 minutes went by as Chuck waited impatiently.

The slowness of the zombies—and the slowness of life in general—was what made the waiting bearable.

When the vehicle—a sturdy forklift—finally built up a full head of steam, Chuck climbed aboard and pulled the throttle down.

Full steam ahead.

The heavy, headless, horseless monster shuddered and lurched forward, smashing through the barn doors of the motorstable.

The stunned security guard shouted, "You can't take that!"

"Try and stop me!" yelled Chuck, flipping him the bird. He pulled the cord that let the steam blow through the steam whistle. It produced a loud, shrill blast.

Chuck's dazed coworkers all looked in his direction.

He began driving in the direction that the zombs had headed. The security guard foolishly ran up to the machine and tried to grab at Chuck's legs. Chuck kicked him in the head and he tumbled away.

The security guard steadied himself on one knee and fired.

The taser darts whizzed past Chuck's head, wrapping around the chimney pipe, discharging sparks of electricity and ripping the weapon from the guard's hand.

"Curse you!" yelled the guard, shaking an angry fist.

chapter 9

The forklift was fast. Fast as about anything available to the public, anyway.

Chuck had not traveled over such a distance at this speed since he was a child. It was the time his pony got stung in the ass by a wasp. He felt as though he were flying. It was a feeling of freedom.

His exhilaration was tempered by his concern for his wife and children. His heart beat loudly.

One's imagination is not one's friend in such situations.

He tried to calm himself. In most of the terrible scenarios that came to his mind, he made them escape. Others he just tried to push out of his mind. Chuck hoped the children would remember that zombies can't climb trees.

He blew through the abandoned Dental Checkpoints.

"Poor bastards," he thought.

He had hoped to get to the schoolhouse before the zombie legion.

But he was too late.

When Chuck pulled up to the school, it was complete pandemonium. The schoolyard appeared to be in the throes of a recess mental breakdown. Clusters of children sobbed in each other's arms. Children randomly sprinted across the campus...or wandered in shock. Teachers, dazed themselves, tried their best to comfort the kids amid the chaos.

Looking over at the paddock, it was clear what had happened. The fence was flattened. Every pony devoured. Nothing left but bones.

* * *

Chuck found his children on the squeaking teeter totter, listlessly going up, and just as listlessly going down. They seemed passive. They were mumbling the names of their dead ponies.

"Butterscotch...Butterscotch...Butterscotch..."

"Butterfly...Butterfly...Butterfly..."

"Come on kids, we are going home."

Charon, who was on the ground end, jumped off the teeter totter.

Asher Lee, who was in the air, came crashing to the ground with a thud. That jolted him out of his stupor.

They quickly ran to their father, clinging to his waist, crying.

Chuck helped the twins up onto the forklift. The twins recounted the terrifying story of a million zombies coming to their school. For some reason, once again, the zombies chose to eat ponies over humans. Strange, indeed.

Once was a fluke. Twice was a pattern.

The zombs had seemingly given up on human flesh and instead had somehow developed a taste for ponies.

Chuck pondered what that might mean.

* * *

The trip home was taken in silence.

The forklift of survivors steamed down the street towards their bucolic home.

When they finally arrived, Jane came running towards them from the house.

"Oh my god. Thank god you're all right. The zombies, they..."

"Mommy!!!"

The twins jumped off the forklift and ran to their mother, grabbing her waist tightly and not letting go. The kids told Jane what had happened at school, sobbing and shaking all over again.

"You were very brave," she told the twins.

Chuck pulled the rig up to the Methane Digester Unit, put the machine into park and hopped off. He adjusted the flame to idle.

"Go in the house and grab your overnight bags," he told the twins. "We're going on a road trip!"

After the kids ran into the house, Jane grabbed Chuck and pressed her mouth into his. She kissed him. Hard. Hugging each other tightly, they made out like they had just survived a zombie apocalypse.

Realizing they didn't have time to fulfill their carnal lust, they pulled themselves apart, straightening their disheveled clothes.

"Honey, they didn't eat the llamas..."

In fact, the zombies seemed quite spooked by them.

"...but they did get Joany, my pony." Tears filled her eyes.

Chuck continued to refill the forklift methane tanks as he pondered that information.

Jane looked at the steam-powered machine and realized a terrible truth.

"Yours, too?" she asked. "Tony...the Pony?"

"I'm afraid so. They ate him like baloney."

He grabbed a few more bottled gas tanks, securing them on the back rack—just in case.

"But why?" she asked. "Why the ponies?"

"I don't know. It makes no sense."

* * *

Chuck entered the house and went to the ice box. He grabbed a jar of cold, fermented pony milk and swilled it down. It hit the spot, in his gut and in his head. He smacked his lips. It had quite a kick to it.

He headed to the living room, where they kept the gun safe. Chuck spun the combination—10-25-38—then swung open the heavy steel door. He reached in and began handing out the heavy weaponry to his family.

AK-47s all around.

They strapped on their sidearms and slung their rifles over their shoulders. Chuck loaded a satchel full of ammo and clips. He grabbed a hand grenade, just to be safe. Then a few more. Just to be extra safe.

Then he went to the closet and took out his head-to-toe zombie-proof kevlar coveralls.

"Just let 'em try and bite me."

They filled everyone's pony cart with weaponry, ammo and provisions. The family had practiced this drill many times before.

They hitched up the llamas to the carts.

They'd been meaning to visit the children's grandparents for a while. Now, with the indefinite shutdown at the plant, it was a perfect excuse for a family outing.

The strange convoy of a lone steam-powered forklift and three llama-drawn pony buggies began down the road, towards the freeway and a showdown with the pony-eating zombies.

* * *

When he was young, Chuck's parents had been eaten. Consequently, he'd been adopted by his grandparents.

As a child, Chuck would travel with his grandfather from town to town. He had a very important part in the traveling show they did together. Chuck's grandfather first warmed up the crowd. He explained the basics of his presentation by flipping through large info panels and charts before presenting a small model of the device, allowing the crowd to appraise its merits in 3-D.

Then Chuck's grandfather would pull the sheet off the magical machine.

A metal wheel, 10 feet in diameter, stood upright and glistened in the sun. He walked up to it and gave it a spin like a carnival wheel of chance. It spun and spun and slowly slowed down.

While continuing his patter, he hopped into the device as it slowed to a predetermined revolution. He started at a brisk trot.

Then he extended his arms and legs in an X and spun around and around. It was like a cartwheel machine.

He did a few other tricky looking moves.

"Round and round it goes, where it stops nobody knows."

He would hop off the thing to great applause.

"So, ladies and gentlemen, you may be asking yourselves, 'Where am I going to find a hamster so large that it will run all day and all night and produce electricity for my home?'

"Well, they don't make them...yet.

"What would you say if I told you that I have here today a creation that will run this electricity -producing turbine wheel all day, all night, every day and every night?!"

The excited crowd was not prepared for what happened next.

"Ladies and gentlemen, let me introduce to you the power source of the future...today!"

Young Chuckie would run up on the stage.

Several people always took it to mean that *he* was the power source of the future.

It never failed to elicit a round of laughter.

Chuck would then run up the stepladder, grab the rope and jump off the ladder with the rope. The rope ran up to a pulley. As he went down, the other sheet was lifted up. The second snap-in portion of the magical power unit was revealed.

The crowd gasped and recoiled. What they saw would make anybody do so.

It was a living, unbreathing zombie, bound and dangling in some strange cage-like construction on wheels.

This was a very tense moment in the show.

The crowd was put on edge just being so close to such a thing. Panic was always a possibility. Everybody knew of someone who had either been killed by one—or turned into one.

One time, in one town, the crowd dispersed and returned with torches and pitchforks before chasing them out of town.

It was up to Little Chuckie to handle the crowd. He ran across the front of the stage and shouted, "Don't worry everybody! This one's tame!"

It was a damn lie.

The crowd laughed away the nervous tension, as they all knew it was a damn lie.

Grandpa rolled the worrisome contraption to the front of the stage. Those in the front row backed up. It was clear that the creature was very secure, but for some reason its arms and legs were free to wave around.

* * *

Little Chuckie then began the real part of his act. He would yell out, "I wuv you, Mr. Zombie!" He would spread his arms wide and run at the dangling monster. He'd grab the zombie's legs and hold them together at the ankles, tightly pressed against his chest. He'd have to use all his weight, lest the zombie kick him in the face.

The smell of the rotting legs was terrible.

His head came up to just under the zombie's knees. The zombie would wildly swing its arms downward, its claws narrowly missing tussling the young lad's hair.

Chuck would hold his breath and count to 10 Mississippi. That was when he was allowed to let go and sidestep out of zombie kicking range.

The crowd applauded.

"See, perfectly safe," claimed Grandpa. Chuckie would then move the ladder right beside the zombie.

"If it wasn't safe, would I let it bite my own grandson?"

Chuckie climbed the ladder. The construction of the restraining device did not allow the zombie to grab him.

When he reached the top of the ladder, Chuckie reached his arm out across the front of the zombie's face.

The zombie clamped its jaw down on Chuck's

forearm.

The crowd went wild, screaming, "No!!!"

Every time it hurt, but he could not let on.

But it would have hurt a lot worse if the zombie had teeth. It also would have turned Chuck into a zombie.

In fact, he had a line he had to deliver: "Ha ha, that tickles."

He would reach over with his right fist, smacking the zombie in the side of the head while yanking his other arm out of the zombie's mouth.

He would then thrust his uneaten arm high in the sky for all to see.

The audience always went wild with applause.

* * *

Grandpa would then continue the demonstration, wheeling the zombie component into the treadmill generator portion.

Once the zombie unit was docked with the hamster wheel unit, Gramps would pour the brain sluice into the brain pan and the magic would begin.

A little fan blew the brain sluice smell towards the zomb. The zomb, smelling the brains, perked right up. It became focused. Single-minded, if you will.

Its decaying nostrils flared, readily detecting the brainy aroma over its own rotting flesh. Its arms floated upward, until they were straight out and shoulder high.

Grandpa turned the crank that gently lowered the already perambulating creature, allowing its feet to make contact with the wheel.

Energy history was being made, one town and country fair at a time.

Chuck loved his grandpa. But, oh, how he hated doing that show. The fact that his parents were killed by zombies made it all the worse. It still gave him terrible nightmares.

chapter 10

It sure would have been great if there was some way to look down from the heavens and get a real-time overview of all those zombie battalions as they made their way down the crumbling highways.

Just imagine if there was still some way to transmit images from outer space. Something along the lines of Google Earth View Live would have been great. This technology, sadly, was no longer possible. Not even Street View.

Even the view from a freaking drone or a traffic copter would have been useful.

This technology was also no longer feasible.

When the Chinese self-replicating space nanobots ran amuck in outer space, they sent every single satellite in orbit crashing to the ground. Communications infrastructure was severely disabled. Satellite TV was a thing of the past, as was GPS.

And when the satellites crashed back to Earth, they brought the nanobots with them—nanobots that didn't particularly care if they were in space or not.

These nanobots were manufactured with a taste for tin and lead. They were made of the stuff and they used it to reproduce themselves. One of the most plentiful and readily accessible sources of these metals was to be found in the circuitry boards of the various electronics around the world.

Once on the ground, the nanobots continued to self-replicate. Soon, billions of these microscopic little fuckers spread out across the globe. They left a wave of nonfunctioning, useless electrical equipment in their wake.

After consuming every military, government and consumer electronics product on the planet, the ravenous bots began to cannibalize their own. Eventually some sort of equilibrium between cannibalization and replication was achieved.

It was another giant step that helped usher along the inevitable adoption of the pony as the predominate means of transportation.

Granted, zeppelins and hot air balloons would have worked just fine as an Early Zombie Warning Defense System. But nobody saw the need.

The real-life, real-time tracking of the undead masses, however, was accomplished by deciphering the panicked Morse code warnings keyed in by the endless network of Dental Checkpoints.

Things had radically changed in the last 100 years.

The borders of the U.S. had been irrevocably altered. When "the Big One" finally hit—a.k.a., The Great FrackQuake of 2040—it was a game changer.

Everything west of the fault dropped below the new sea level. As the middle of America chunk of the continent rose, the eastern and western seaboards went under. California? Gone. New York City? Gone. Washington, D.C.? Gone.

Tens of millions of wicked Americans drowned for their wickedness.

The entertainment industry? Gone. Silicon Valley? Gone. Wall Street? Gone. The federal government? Gone.

All gone.

* * *

It looked like tectonics had foiled the President's plans to reunite Pangea.

Those that were not killed outright began a great mass migration inland. Detroit, once a foundering and dying city, had a renaissance. She saw a tripling of the population. The construction trades flourished, as did the local economy. Thousands of new homes were built to accommodate the influx of refugees. New Detroit became a leader in manufacturing and technology and the arts.

During the transition, there was a time in the Remaining United States of Upper America when it was mad scientists who received the largest portion of the nation's defense budget.

Losing the East and West Coast was a huge brain drain on the nation. Both coasts had harbored the cream of the crop in terms of scientific and military minds. Now Silicon Valley and the Pentagon lay in ruins under the sea.

America had to rely on the remaining heartland of America to fill its scientific and military needs. Not to mention its entertainment needs.

It was time for America's second string to step up.

It was from this pool that Dr. Zakk Von Flash—of Dr. Zakk Von Flash, *Electric Zombie Boogaloo* fame—rose. Originally, he operated along the lines of a traveling snake oil show. Traveling the county fair circuit with his grandson Chuck, he made a presentation that touted the utility and entertainment value of installing Home Zombie Energy Turbine Units.

Dr. Von Flash would take some orders and local contractors would install the prefab units. Four to six weeks later, a genuine zombie—or two or three, depending on the model unit—would arrive, thanks to the recently federalized Fed Ex.

* * *

Dr. Zakk Von Flash, the pioneering scientist who first implanted electrodes into the zombies, was widely admired and was taught in high schools and universities alongside the likes of Alexander Graham Bell and Nikola Tesla.

Dr. Von Flash's hilarious proof of concept demonstration consisted of using a remote controller to make a zombie recreate the dance routine from Michael Jackson's *Thriller* video.

For the guys in the lab, it was a crackup. Before long, a leaked cell phone video went viral.

All that publicity led to a successful appearance on the TV show *Shark Tank*. All of the celebrity capital investors wanted in.

Production was ramped up and the concept scaled exponentially. In no time at all, a working Zombie Turbine prototype was created and a new age was ushered in.

Someone had finally found the answer to the age old question: "What are we gonna do with all these gosh darn zombies?"

Part of the national PSYOP campaign to acclimate Americans to zombie power included the *Electric Zombie Boogaloo*. This was Dr. Von Flash's popular touring musical zombie review.

The crowds were electrified—as were the zombies.

There were also several zombie-themed situation comedies on the air. *Honey, the Zombies Ate the Kids* was quite popular. The toddler zombie's catch phrase whine, "I want braayaaiiiinsss," swept the nation.

The Super Bowl commercial was a brilliant mind-changer in the public's attitude towards zombie energy and zombies in general. The spot included the recently re-animated corpse of Michael Jackson, plus a cast of real-life zombies, recreating the dance routine from the *Thriller* video, move for move.

After the dance was over, the zombies—led by zombie Michael Jackson—made their way to a Zombie Energy Turbine Facility. They then proceed to cheerfully strap themselves into their harnesses and begin their endless task of energy production.

The shoot was arduous and took numerous weeks to complete. No matter how many electrodes you implant, zombie dancers are considerably less fluid than their living counterparts.

But folks who would have never gotten along in everyday life would work side by side for eternity, towards a common goal, for the greater good—or at least until their legs fell off from wear and tear and decomposition.

They were heady times, when anything seemed possible.

* * *

The Hesson family made their way towards the freeway. The llamas trotted double time to keep up with the forklift.

As the steam-powered machine chugged along steadily, Chuck wondered why everybody didn't travel this way. It was a beautiful day for a family adventure. There was a mystery to be solved and they were just the family to try and sort it out.

Chuck and his brood could tell they were getting closer as the terrible smell intensified. Every time the wind shifted, there was the overpowering stench of death.

Chuck was fairly used to it, thanks to his long years at the plant. In fact, it reminded him of all the good times he and his grandfather had experienced together.

"That stink? That's the smell of money!"

Grandpa would always say.

But the kids and Jane—they'd retch every time it blew in their direction.

Every so often they would see a twitching, rotted limb in the road. If it was a rotted leg, you could be sure there'd be a crawling zombie not too far ahead.

The twins argued over who would get to take the head shot.

"Kids, kids, kids...there will be plenty of zombies for everyone," Jane said as she pulled her llama cart up to the crippled crawling zombie.

She unholstered her sidearm, took aim and pulled the trigger, blowing the zombie's skull and all its contents all over the road.

"Now, why don't you kids find a nice way to decide who gets the next one."

"Awww, okay, Ma."

They finally agreed on the game rock/paper/scissors as the final arbiter. Two out of three.

The family followed the zombie horde onto the onramp. The overpass afforded a startling overview of the highway below and into the distance. The magnitude of the day sunk in.

Stretching into the distance, every few miles from every direction, was another 5000-strong legion of the undead. All marching in lockstep towards New Detroit.

Each legion was the entire zombie workforce of an entire ZTF.

It was a full-scale zombie revolution.

* * *

Chuck thought to himself—"It makes little or no sense."

He turned it over and over in his mind. In his brain, he replayed the unbelievably choreographed events on the turbine floor. Slowly, he began to piece it together.

"Well, if it wasn't an *accidental* release...the claim of no accidental escapes still stands."

Always the company man, that Chuck. It wasn't the first time he'd been called a shill.

Would the Zombie Energy Industry ever recover from this—whatever *this* was? A wildcat strike against their enslavement? An uprising?

Whatever it was, it wasn't good. It wasn't good for ponies. It wasn't good for America.

It was certainly a mass migration, if nothing else. A wonder, if not of nature, of something else.

His thoughts were interrupted by the sound of short automatic gunfire bursts. The Hesson kids had giddily opened fire from the overpass onto the zombies below.

"Die, zombies, die!" they screamed.

"Kids! Knock it off!"

"Awww. But we're having a first-person zombie shooter contest."

"Save your ammo, kids. We might need it."

* * *

Not only had they been following behind a

zombie legion, but Chuck and his family also had a zombie legion following behind them—probably several more behind them, in fact. Maybe several more in front of them, too.

There were thousands of identical ZTFs in the region. If they had all malfunctioned along the lines of Chuck's, there could be hundreds of thousands of zombs converging in their direction.

This new understanding of their present situation necessitated some discussion. The new zombie behaviors observed that day were a major factor in the consideration.

Traditionally, zombs did not march in formation. They never worked well together in the wild. They were more all willie nillie and pel mel— every zomb for themselves.

And before today, zombies only wanted to eat living humans. Other animals were not considered a food source. But today they turned their nostrils up at warm, living humans. It was ponies only on the menu.

Chuck didn't like to brag. He had a Masters in Zombology. He had earned it.

But all his education had not prepared him for this. Maybe there had been a rip in the space-time continuum. It is true that some days seemed *very* different than the day before.

Maybe the sky was a different color...or you suddenly found that you had an extra finger. It was always something. But you could never really put your extra finger on it. There were no memories of how it was different from the day before, because it was just like today.

As the day wore on, the feeling that somehow something had changed faded like a dream.

Perhaps this was the new normal. If the new normal was a constant, they had little to worry about. In terms of getting eaten, at least.

If this was an alternate reality, it might stand to reason that there should be no memories of how things had changed from the day before, because in such a case, things would have always been that way.

Therefore, they had to assume this was not an alternate reality glitch created by some time traveler fuck up.

Unless, of course, that was the very nature of this alt reality. A reality where things could change radically from the day before and you would be totally aware of the changes.

That seemed like a terrible type of reality—a reality where the rug could be pulled out from under your feet at a moment's notice. A reality where you always had to be on your toes.

Could such a radical change in zombie behavior just occur overnight?

It sure seemed that way.

It was true that zombies hadn't been observed in the wild for a very long time. Perhaps it was their very domestication that changed them.

Had the years marching side by side on the treadmills made them like that?

* * *

Chuck and Jane felt they were presently in no immediate danger. If they had felt otherwise, they would never have endangered their two children so recklessly.

Sure, the kids had received their anti-zombie bite vaccinations. But that would not help them if they were torn apart and eaten by zombies.

Granted, there were about 5000 zombies directly ahead of them about three-quarters of a mile in the distance—plus another 5000 or so directly behind them.

So if everyone kept their present pace, they'd remain exactly between both legions of zombs. There was plenty of time and plenty of places where they could ditch off the highway and head for the hills.

chapter 11

For those too young to remember...

King Kong was a prehistoric 50-foot-tall stop-motion gorilla. He was captured on Skull Island by the impresario Carl Denham in 1933. The gargantuan gorilla was then transported to New York City for exhibition.

On opening night, a tuxedoed Denham introduced the hulking primate to dazzled New Yorkers.

"And now, ladies and gentlemen, before I tell you any more, I'm going to show you the greatest thing your eyes have ever beheld. He was a king and a god in the world he knew, but now he comes to civilization merely a captive—a show to gratify your curiosity. Ladies and gentlemen, behold the mighty Kong—the Eighth Wonder of the World!"

The photo bulbs flashed as the media captured the moment. Kong, predictably and on cue, went berserk.

He escaped his shackles, kidnapped his interspecies love interest, film star Fay Wray, and climbed to the top of the Empire State Building. He got shot down both by airplanes and Fay Wray on the same night, falling 100 stories to his death. Kong died of massive internal injuries.

Luckily, he set Fay Wray down before falling. She had a story to dine out on for the rest of her life.

Denham wasn't so lucky. The City of New York sued his holding company. As luck—or speculation, as some speculated—would have it, Denham had taken out a very large insurance policy in the event of just such an event.

The City of New York was satisfied that it would be reimbursed and withdrew its lawsuit. But the families of the 26 civilians killed by Kong during his rampage launched a civil suit.

Denham maintained it was an act of God. Detractors claimed it was he who was acting as God, bringing that giant monkey into the city.

Denham claimed the exorbitant insurance policy was all for publicity and that he had no intention of releasing the terrible beast on the public. But there were those who questioned this claim. Some of the public questioned the integrity of the restraints and backup shackles.

The only charges ever brought against Denham amounted to "creating a civil disorder." The investigation into the events of the King Kong rampage found no official wrongdoing.

In an effort to cut his losses, the promoter made the exciting public announcement that he would be creating a limited line of luxury fur coats and fur-lined accessories—made from the hide of the fallen King Kong.

Kong's carcass had already been shipped to Michigan by refrigerated rail car. Denham had sold Kong to Henry Ford, who was experimenting with cryogenic freezing in his lab. The two men shook hands and smacked their lips as they signed their mutual non-disclosure agreement.

* * *

With such notoriety fresh in the public's mind, the country experienced a small 'King Kong hide' boom. Denham had thousands of pre-orders— more orders than he could have ever delivered after skinning and tanning King Kong's jumbo hide.

But that didn't bother Carl Denham one bit.

He had already lined up dozens of Japanese furrier factories to produce the items. He also bought several herds of yaks. His workaround was simple enough: He trademarked the process of dying Yak fur a distinctive monkey black shade, then adding a good solid monkey stank.

He called the finished product—'King Kong Miracle Hide.'

Henry Ford, himself, had some wild idea of bringing Kong back to life and selling him to the Nazis as a super weapon. That Henry Ford, he was some sort of character.

Eventually, Ford gave up such foolish ideas. The lab was abandoned and Kong languished in his industrial freezer for more than 150 years.

When urban explorers discovered the massive underground chambers years later, there was much tabloid excitement.

* * *

These were heady times.

The zombie outbreaks were almost controlled. The Flying Winged Monkey Project was sailing right ahead. Pony engineering was providing all sorts of breakthroughs. It seemed like there was nothing that these best and brightest—or what was left of them, anyway—could not do.

One of their most audacious projects was the attempt to re-animate the corpse of King Kong.

This was as terrible an idea that could possibly be conceived.

Using infusions of recombinant zombie DNA, the mad scientist government industrial complex hacks immediately went to work making Henry Ford's dream a reality—the part about re-animating Kong, not so much the part about selling off Kong to the Nazis.

Once their long struggle finally came to fruition, everybody involved in the project immediately regretted it.

The re-animation was a success.

But the moment after his eyes fluttered open, Kong's massive head and maw lunged forward. Before anyone could stop him, he had bitten three technicians in half.

* * *

They came from Ann Arbor on 94. From Toledo and Monroe, north along former Interstate 75, they marched. From the north and from the east, they came across on Highway 94. Down the Chrysler Highway. Down John Lodge.

They came across U.S. Route 85 to W. Fort Street. Down Woodward, down John Sinclair Avenue. From Lansing on I-96, on to the Fisher Freeway merging onto 75 and leading directly into the heart of the new U.S. Capitol, they marched.

New Detroit was surrounded.

The zombies came to the unfinished weather dome—a.k.a., the 25-foot wall that protected the city. They repeated their undead human pyramid trick and were soon climbing over the impediment as easily as army ants—once again leaving a large crushed pile of their wriggling comrades behind.

"Zombie alert! Update! City limits
have been breached.
Remain at your workstations.
Please standby for further updates."

The pronouncement echoed through the city's PA system.

New Detroit had become the New Zombie Mecca and all the zombies were making a pilgrimage. Any zombie that was any zombie was sure to be there. It was a zombie Woodstock. The zombie Summer of Love.

If you're shambling to New Detroit, be sure to

wear some rotting meat in your hair.

* * *

The zombies approached the Capitol complex of Fort RenCen of New Detroit. The sky grew dark with thousands of genetically-mutated flying winged monkeys.

They were also known as tooth faeries.

The beasts were America's first line of defense against domestic terrorists and protesters. Up until this time, the FWMs had only been used for Urban Dental Law Enforcement and Domestic Crowd Control Operations. They had never squared off with a zombie army before.

There never was a zombie army before.

The flying winged monkeys circled the Renaissance Towers in a protective halo. They tightly gripped their two-foot-long, electric-shock-inducing toothbrush/riot batons.

Nervous monkey chatter echoed in the wind—while a steady stream of flying winged monkey poop showered the streets from above.

* * *

As the Hesson family approached the downtown area, the zombie ranks pulled in tighter. At one point, there was less than a city block between the zombs in the front and the zombs in the rear.

A block or so after this realization, Chuck made a left-hand turn signal and led his little convoy down a sidestreet.

Halfway down the street, the Hessons took a right down the alley. Chuck and his family could see the last mile was a straight shot, free of zombies.

"Does anybody have to go the bathroom?"

They stopped and relieved themselves—Jane and Charon on one side of the alley, Chuck and Asher on the other. Zipping and pulling up their britches, they also realized that the alley behind them allowed a clear and free exit.

"What does everyone want to do?"

"Kill more zombies!!!" the children screamed.

"They killed Butterscotch!" screamed Asher, shaking his fist in the air.

"...and Butterfly!!!" added Charon, shaking her fist in the air.

"...and Joany!!!" screamed Jane, joining in the fist shaking.

"...and Tony!!!" yelled Chuck, with his version of the shaking fist.

It's true that humans had hunted zombies for sport for about as long as zombies had been hunting humans.

This time, though, it was personal.

* * *

Jane and Chuck had been meaning to take the kids on a family trip to see the Capital Fortress of the R.U.S.U. of A. for quite some time. It would be a shame to have to miss it after getting so close.

They could see the towers. It was a clear shot

to the plaza. They could always turn around if it got too hairy. The tours were probably not operating, but maybe the gift shop would be open.

Jane half-remembered a giant dancing monkey behind a wall of solid glass. Out of all the lab mutation experiments, the flying winged monkeys were truly a crowning achievement. To be able to create— and then clone—these beasts by the thousands was truly outstanding!

The FWM Project was given a high priority by the first Supreme administration. It was second on the list only to the Pony ID Project.

Unlike the Pony Manhattan Project, however, the FWM Project was completely **Top Secret**.

There were rumors circulating that Shriners had been rounded up by the thousands during one of the dictator's many pogroms. This one was specifically engineered to seize their supply of fezzes.

* * *

From high above, the FWMs began their assault on the invaders. They swooped down from the sky, buzzing over the heads in the crowd. They were beating their wings, showing their fangs and howling. They beat and shocked the zombies about the head and shoulders.

But the zombies barely looked up.

The fear that the flying winged monkeys were so easily able to elicit from humans was completely absent in the zombies. The standard issue electric cattle prod toothbrush batons had little or no effect on the zombs.

The monkeys unleashed one of their more terrifying tricks. Pairs of six-foot-tall monkeys dropped out of the sky, grabbing random individuals from the crowd by the shoulders and snatching them up into the clouds.

Normally, this would create utter panic and chaos in a crowd.

The zombs, however, were completely non-plussed.

Not only that, but the zombs being taken for a flight were trying to viciously bite their winged monkey captors.

What would a flying winged monkey zombie look like? Strangely, this was one question that the scientists had failed to ask.

Perhaps today they would find out.

* * *

Jane wondered if they might see any celebrity memes. She wished she had thought to bring her pinhole camera. She remembers the first time she saw the Fortress of America, during a class trip. She'd had her picture taken with the preserved corpse of revered meme-man, Tron Guy.

There were many stuffed meme corpses in the refurbished Smithsonian Hall of Heroes on the fourth floor of Building Two. All the nations' most meaningful cultural artifacts had been lost during the Great FrackQuake. The Smithsonian did the best it could with what it could lay its hands on.

The Hessons approached the next cross street. They were about 10 feet from their destination when a sudden flood of zombies—a hideous zomb parade—burst across the street ahead, blocking their way.

Slowly, the Hessons cautiously chugged up to the intersection. The forklift was flanked by the kids' carts, pulled by a team of llamas, who hissed at the zombies.

Before long, all pandemonium broke loose. The zombies went crazy. Snorting and shrieking, they spun around on their heels and jumped back.

It was the closest thing to zombie panic that Chuck had ever seen.

They cautiously inched forward. It was as if they had discovered some amazing new zombie repellant technology.

Was it the steam engine forklift? Was it the team of spitting llamas? Or was it a combination of the two?

Either way, they were not going to conduct a scientific study at that moment to find out. The llamas obviously hated the zombies. They strained mightily against their reigns.

But the zombies parted for the llamas—or maybe it was the forklift—like the Red Sea parted for Moses.

chapter 12

The top three floors of the RenCen were still a very nice rotating restaurant. But it was no longer open to the public.

From its dizzying height, one could almost see from sea to shining sea. It served as a cafeteria to the public bureaucrat drones serving their country. The first 50 floors—once a luxury hotel—had been converted into Level One government employee office housing. If you lived here, you would be at work right now, forever.

The RenCen, as it had always been known to the denizens of Detroit, covered 14 acres. The centerpiece was a 73-floor circular tower, surrounded by four 39-story office towers (100-400) and two 21-story buildings (500-600). A 10-foot wall had been constructed around the perimeter to keep out the unwashed masses.

The Renaissance Center had become the bureaucratic hub of the federated government of the Remaining United States of Upper America

(R.U.S.U.A.). It had once been owned by General Motors (GM).

During the transition times, in accordance with a decree from the High Council of Internet Memes, General Motors had been nationalized and redubbed General Ponies. Once upon a time, what was good for General Motors was good for America.

Now the boot was on the other foot.

* * *

A cantilevered addition to the top 10 stories of the tallest building—the central tower that had no number—was added to make the skyscraper approximate the upside down boot of sainted warrior Vermin Supreme.

The addition extended 75 feet. Retrofitting such a cantilever onto the pre-existing skyscraper was no mean feat. The engineering and execution of this glorious boot toe extension was sketchy, at best. Architects and engineers, like every other profession in America, had lost the best and the brightest in the earthquakes and tsunamis.

The second tier were suddenly the best in their fields.

The 20 floors above the bureaucrats—and below the restaurant—were something else indeed. Each circular floor contained row after concentric row of plexiglass shelves that ran from floor to ceiling. Each shelving unit held 12 shelves, with rows spaced four feet apart, allowing comfortable passage for technicians and cleaning crews.

Let's see...the circular tower was 188 feet in diameter...divide by four...47 divided by two...23 concentric circles of shelves. Round it down to twenty to account for the width of the shelves themselves and the elevator shaft. Multiply times 12, the number of shelves...times 20 stories.

And that's just the shelves themselves.

On each shelf, a slightly curved row of 20 large identical glass jars, side by side, were connected by tubing and wiring. The jars were wider than they were tall, each with its own thermometer.

Hundreds of Windex-wielding illegal Canadian prisoners of war worked around the clock to dust and polish the endless shelves of glass jars. Dressed in red jumpsuits and wearing shock collars, they were unfailingly polite to everyone they'd meet.

Technicians in lab coats and clipboards walked up and down the aisles, pointing and taking notes, checking off boxes on the various forms. Occasionally, they'd wiggle one of the many wires that ran between the vessels. Their conversations were in hushed tones, as in a hospital or library. The lighting was muted.

Each vessel was filled with a clear nutrient solution. Oxygen bubbles percolated up from the bottom.

Floating...

...one in each jar...

...was a healthy human brain.

From each brain, a number of multi-colored wires connected it to the brain in the next jar. Tubing ran behind the brains, providing the much-needed oxygen and nutrients.

Little fish swam around, keeping the tanks free of waste.

These were the cloned brains of Emperor Vermin Supreme.

The brains pulsated. Working together, their vast number comprised a living super-computer.

These were the brains that ruled the country.

They must be protected at any cost.

* * *

From the horrified viewpoint of the onlookers in the high-rise fortress, it looked like some epic battle was underway. In reality, the elite simian squadrons may as well have been mosquitoes. The once fearsome flying winged monkey squadrons were rendered ineffective, barely a nuisance to the zombie hoard.

The loud feminine voices echoing over the PA system were bland and reassuring.

"Please return to your work stations.
Everything is under control.
There is nothing to see outside."

Chuck's family slowly proceeded into the intersection, crossing the raging river of zombies.

Fluid zombie dynamics seemed to rule. The Hessons were in a bubble. They had a zombie-free zone surrounding them, a circle some 15 feet in radius. Chuck took point. Jane took the rear. The kids took their respective sides. They each had their weapons set on full auto, leveled and scanning their respective quadrant.

They practiced their drill.

Clockwise they went.

"12 o'clock—clear."

"Three o'clock—clear."

"Six o'clock—clear."

"Nine o'clock—clear."

As they had been taught, the kids used great firearms discipline. Their trigger finger pressed tight against the body of the rifle. They'd been told very sternly—"No more zombie shooting without permission."

* * *

The Hessons made it to the other side of the street and into the alley. Relieved, invigorated and pumped with adrenaline, they jumped out of their carts and off the steam-powered forklift and shook out their arms and legs.

They soon wrapped themselves into a family group hug and checked in.

"I don't think the zombies like us."

"They were afraid of us!"

"Did you see them run?"

"Is everybody ok?"

"Do we want to continue?"

The kids nodded their heads up and down.

"Who wants to see Fort America?!"

They looked behind them at the torrent of

zombs. They looked up and forward to the sun shining through the clouds and down on the towers. Their gaze returned to the Earth. Ahead they saw a plaza pulsating with zombies.

"In for a dime, in for a pony," Jane said.

Each street they'd cross would require a look to the left and to the right. The streets running parallel to the alley were full of one-way zombie rush hour traffic headed toward the Windsor River.

A block away from the Hessons, another zombie tributary burst across the nearest cross street. Confident and committed, the family went full steam ahead. And once again, the zombies backed off as they had before.

Successfully crossing the street, they found the last block of alley full of zombie overspill from the plaza.

The Hessons continued on, undaunted—while the panicked zombies flattened themselves against the alley walls. They couldn't get enough space between themselves and the humans.

And it was a very long block.

Finally, the family came out the other side, into the sunshine and more zombies. The magnitude of being the only humans in a crowded plaza slowly sunk in.

The Hessons entered the plaza and headed towards the walls of the fortress. Hoping to get a better view, Chuck raised the platform extending on the forklift. He brought it up to the same level as the roof and put the vehicle in park.

He climbed up onto the roof, then helped

Jane and the children up onto the perch. They stood up and marveled at the sight of so many zombies in all directions.

The zombs maintained their distance.

* * *

The giant service access doors to Fort RenCen swung open and the troop carriers rolled out. The gates of the troop carriers opened and the troops marched down the ramps, into formation.

Then the giant service access doors to Fort RenCen swung closed behind them, locked and secured.

Wearing a stylized helmet that was somewhere between boot and Roman Centurion, the marshal addressed the palace guards.

"Men, today we live and die for the Emperor. You have sacrificed much to make it here today, and you are willing to sacrifice it all here today. You are the cream of all the surgical soldiers. Hell, you are the few that were brave enough to step up when your country called.

"Soon, your endless hours of training will be put to the test."

It was refreshing to have an enemy that was literally not human. There was no time nor brain space wasted on dehumanizing them. They were already dehumans.

"Remember," shouted the marshal, "our enemy today is not human!!!...Our enemies today are already dead!!!

"Every one that you kill today is for the good of the country—and the good of the creatures themselves. Their families will thank you. Whoever has the highest kill rate today will get extra rations...and a furlough...to the red light zone...

"You are here today because you are the best of the best human-pony hybrids that this country has ever known."

* * *

"Soldier, if you see your grandmother out there today, what are you going to do?"

"Kill her, sir."

"I can't HEAR you!"

"KILL HER, SIR!"

"That's better. And if you see your sister here today? What are you going to do?"

"KILL HER, SIR!"

Why these men had volunteered to have their own human bottom parts surgically removed and be attached to pony bodies was anybody's guess. But they had, hundreds of them, and now they were ready to defend their country's Capitol from the advancing zombs.

"Sarge, I'm scared."

"Of course you are. You'd be a fool not to be."

"Steady...steady, men...steady," the sergeant said calmly.

"Don't toot 'til you see the yellowy whites of their eyes," he told the trumpeter.

Then the commander sergeant centaur gave

the order to the manponies.

"Charge!!!"

Swinging their swords and battle axes furiously, the Centaur Cavalry attacked. The ponymen charged headlong into the pulsating zombie mob.

Zombie heads flew. Zombie heads rolled. Headless zombie bodies collapsed to the ground.

By the score, they fell.

Zombie limbs lopped off by the hundreds. The ponymen's weapons were cutting through the crowd like butter. Zombies had not evolved an unnatural defense against this new sword-wielding predator. Things were going swimmingly for the troops.

The carnage was horrifying.

They cut a wide swath deep into the undead legions. The sheer massive number of zombies, however, assured that they would be, eventually, surrounded.

Sure enough, they were.

When this occurred there was a predictable turn of events. The equi-humans were no longer on the offense. What was once going great was now... not so great.

The Centaur Cavalry formed a defensive circle—several, actually—as this was happening throughout the plaza.

But the never-ending onslaught of zombies finally became too much. Their defensive circles became compacted and too crowded to even use their weapons effectively.

The zombies, who had seemingly mutated into not eating humans, realized that the humans who were busy severing their heads were also half delicious pony.

As the centaurs reared up to get more kicking action, zombies clamped themselves to the tender pony underbellies and began to bite and rip thru their hide. Zombies wrapped themselves around the centaurs' legs, weighing them down to be eaten by the throng. Some centaurs rolled on their backs to try and shake off the zombies.

Nothing seemed to work.

Discipline broke down amongst the troops. It became every ponyman for himself.

HAGEN-BRENNER

chapter 13

The zombies continued to swarm.

They piled on and began feasting on the pony portion of the centaurs. They were eating them alive!!!

Curiously, the zombs left the upper human portions uneaten, leaving the centaurs to die in agony. Needless to say, under the circumstances of their demise, they themselves would be squirming, legless zombies before the end of the day.

Not a single centaur survived the battle that day. Years later there would be a plaque commemorating their bravery. Rest their souls.

The zombies swarmed Hart Plaza, quickly filling to its 40,000 person capacity. They descended around the sculpture titled: 'The Monument to (boxer) Joe Louis.' The monument was also known as 'The Fist.' It was commissioned by the meme content conglomerate Time Inc. for the city of New Detroit, known back then simply as 'Detroit.'

Unveiled in the late 20th century, The Monument to Joe Louis was a 24-foot long arm ending with a defiant fist. Zombies swarmed around and underneath the 8,000-pound bronze Joe Louis arm. They lifted the massive sculpture, looking like some sort of millipede. They began to slowly turn the fist around and around until the cables, tethering it to its steel I-beam frame, snapped.

'The Brown Bomber,' as Joe Louis was known, helped shatter the Nazi myth of racial superiority with his dramatic defeat of German champion Max Schmeling during the rise of Nazism. Due to his love for ponies, Louis served in a segregated cavalry unit during World War II. When commenting on the fact of segregation, Louis famously said, "Lots of things wrong with America, but Hitler ain't going to fix them."

Joe Louis was one of the greatest heavyweight world champions of all time. He also broke the color barrier on the PGA golf tour. Truly a great hero of the pre-zombified, pre-ponytopia America.

Because of Joe Louis' role in smashing through the color barrier, Mexican-American sculptor Robert Graham referred to his creation as a 'battering ram.' He had no idea how accurate this description would turn out to be.

* * *

The zombies may not have known what art is, but they seemed to know what they liked. They seemed to like this massive object very much.

The zombs started passing the hand—hands

over heads—crowdsurfing the four-ton arm. The giant disembodied Joe Louis fist began to pick up speed and inertia as it sailed over the sea of zombies down Jefferson Avenue.

The flying winged monkeys were unable to stop the progress of the gigantic forearm as it flew down Jefferson Ave. towards the nation's bureaucratic Capitol Fortress.

The Centaur Cavalry, still fighting to the death, were unable to assist. The Hessons, standing atop their forklift platform, were slack-jawed as they saw the giant fist fly by.

The government workers in the tower pressed their faces against the glass to get a better look. There were zombies as far as the eye could see. The workers looked down upon the sculpted fist of mighty Joe Louis moving down the street toward the fort. Seen from above, it looked exactly what you might imagine.

Every eye followed the fist below as it moved quickly towards them.

They collectively gasped as it easily smashed through the giant service access gate of the palace fortress. They could see the zombies pouring into the courtyard through the open gates—the very courtyard that held everybody's ponies!!!

The marauding zombies began their horrible feast.

"Zombie alert update.
Fortress gate has been breached.
Palace courtyard has been overrun.

Please remain at your workstations. Thank you.
Stand by for further updates."

Their eyes widened as the flying fist disappeared under their feet. The massive hand of Joe Louis came smashing through the glass wall of the giant atrium and into the lobby. Sheets of glass rained down like confetti. The few humans in the lobby ran for the stairs.

As always, the muzak version of The Themesong of America played in the background.

The zombie-powered fist, having picked up much momentum, continued through the lobby at an incredible rate of speed. It easily destroyed the receptionist/information/security kiosk and continued through the vast atrium, towards the giant glass cage that just happened to house one of the most fearsome creatures on the planet.

Behind that three-inch thick glass was Zombie King Kong.

*   *   *

The only thing between the three-inch glass wall and the flying megabronze fist of Joe Lewis was the gift shop. The gift shop had many wonderful tchotchkes and gewgaws. There were holographic Vermin Supreme bobbleheads. Vermin Supreme snow globes. Plush Zombie King Kong dolls. There were shot glasses, mirrors and bomber jackets with the heavy metal-style ZKK logo. There was a whole section dedicated to pony stuff. Conspicuously absent—zombie swag.

The cashier looked on in slow motion as the fist obliterated her beloved store and hit the wall of Kong's enclosure. The glass cube shattered, the fist clipping Kong. It spun him around and knocked him on his ass.

The fist continued its trajectory and ripped through the back wall, hitting one of the building's supporting columns with such force that the entire skyscraper shook. Giant chunks of jagged glass crushed dozens of zombies in the lobby, cutting some gratuitously right in half, lengthwise—in seemingly slow motion.

King Kong had been a fearsome greeter to all who visited Fort RenCen Capital Tower since shortly after he was re-animated. There wasn't much else to do with him.

Zombie Kong was too dangerous. He was uncontrollable. Unpredictable. May as well put him on display—like a monster, a living Vladimir Lenin.

* * *

Kong pulled himself up, off his ass, and proceeded to go full on zombie apeshit. He started jumping up and down and beating his chest. Every time he landed, he smooshed several zombies. He rolled around furiously on the ground, crushing zombies by the dozen.

Kong ran in circles around the lobby, picking up speed. He bounced from wall to wall, his massive bulk breaking through the marble façade, exposing the I-beams underneath. He started picking zombies up by the fist-full and throwing them against the wall. He was merciless.

Bronzed, rested and entering on his back, RoboCop suddenly and incongruously appeared.

But this wasn't the fictional futuristic crime fighter himself. Rather, it was the 10-foot bronze statue depicting the fictional futuristic crime fighter of 1980's movie fame. The zombs had pulled down the statue like it was that of an overthrown tyrant, then crowdsurfed it over their heads into the lobby. The statue, being much lighter than the Joe Louis bronze fist, moved much faster.

It was not slowed down by having to break through the gate of the fortress. So by the time it arrived in the lobby, the 10-foot bronze statue was moving as fast as a steam locomotive. Kong leapt out of the way as the speeding, Kickstarter-funded RoboCop statue flew headfirst through the wall of elevators. Meeting little resistance, he continued and hit another center-supporting column. The impact made a mighty ding.

The building trembled as the powerful shock ran up the tower. Tens of thousands of the building's occupants broke into a subtle panic. The High Council of Internet Memes on floor 53 proposed an emergency declaration condemning the current situation.

Kong grabbed the RoboCop statue by the ankles and pulled it out of the hole in the wall in which it was lodged. He swung the statue around and around the vast lobby, destroying everything that had not been destroyed yet.

"Zombie alert update. Palace lobby has been
breached. The building is now in lockdown.
Please remain at your workstations.
Everything is under control.
Stand by for further updates.
Smile and have a nice day."

After beating at the walls for a while, Kong swung the statue upward at the ceiling with much force. RoboCop's face easily broke through the ceiling into the next floor. Humans and furniture came tumbling down from above. Kong found that somewhat exciting, so he swung the battering statue again through another spot.

More furniture and humans fell from the ceiling like a piñata.

*   *   *

It was at this unfortunate moment that the basic zombie behavioral lever was somehow reset. The zombs gave up on their distaste for humans.

Suddenly, the zombies were viciously devouring the unlucky humans falling into their midst.

Smash!!! Smash!!! Smash!!! Again and again Kong swung the statue, hitting the same spot several times while creating a hole large enough for him to crawl up into.

Kong leapt up, catching himself on the edge of the gaping hole. He was able to squeeze his head—then his arm and shoulder—up into the next floor.

He scooped up terrified humans and stuffed them into his foaming maw.

Meanwhile, the zombies continued to flood into the lobby. They poured into the exposed elevator shafts. Most fell down the shaft, while some climbed the cables. The elevator shaft began to fill with bodies. Soon, they filled the entire atrium, climbing over each other, three deep.

The damn zombies were everywhere. Bursting through the doors to the stairwells, a steady stream of zombs continuing to go up the upstairs and down the down stairs.

They quickly filled the basement floors and began to fill the first floor above the atrium. As more zombies filled the floor, many were being pushed into the gaping holes in the floor that Kong had made. Zombies fell from the ceiling—along with the occasional terrified human—into an ocean of the undead, five zombies deep.

Zombs began to cling to Kong's legs, climbing him. This caused Kong to jump up and down with great force, shaking off some zombies and crushing many more in the process.

* * *

Looking outside, Kong realized there was more to his kingdom than just an atrium full of zombies. Using the holes he punched in the ceiling as grab holds, he swung across the lobby and leapt outside. He landed with a mighty squish, almost slipping and losing his balance on the squirmy zombie pâté underneath his feet.

He beat his chest in typical monster ape fashion and let out a mighty roar. Kong was energized by his newfound freedom.

In the middle of the pulsating zombie mass, he saw the family of humans, huddled on a platform. They appeared to be an edible, tasty plate of humans just waiting to be eaten.

Kong started monkey-jumping through the sea of zombs, his giant monkey feet crushing zombies with every step.

As soon as the Hessons saw this huge zombie ape coming their way, they did not hesitate. Immediately it was: ready, steady, aim and...*fire!*

Team Hesson lit up ol' Zombie Kong like a Christmas tree. The last time Kong caught hot lead like that was on top of the Empire State Building over a century ago. The gunfire brought back vivid monkey memories. Kong could see the tracers as he dove and monkey-rolled through the zombies. He jumped up in the sky and landed, then cartwheeled and did other evasive monkey maneuvers as he tried to evade the stinging pellets.

The Hessons did not understand yet that this giant ape was also a zombie—a zombie that was already dead!!!

The great ape had no blood to bleed. It had no functional vital organs that could be destroyed by bullets. The ape somersaulted and skidded to a stop, flat on its back, mere yards from the Hessons.

Kong, easily distracted and in no hurry, paused and took a moment to catch his zombie breath. He looked up at the sky, cloudy and blue, and felt the breeze blow through his fur. He began to notice the squirming magic finger zombie massage he was receiving on his underside.

The Hesson family looked down upon the motionless ape. It wasn't breathing. They naturally assumed they'd killed the great beast with their superior firepower.

But as anyone who's ever seen a horror or monster movie would know, that was a terrible thing to assume.

The Hessons took a moment for a group hug, unaware that things were about to get real crazy all over again.

chapter 14

No one alive would have ever noticed the resemblance. But with his long blond hair and feminine
features, Chuck vaguely resembled his great-great-
great grandmother, the silent movie star Fay Wray.

It's unlikely that anyone dead, for that matter, would have noticed the resemblance. But to the
recently-freed Kong—with his terrible zombie eye-
sight—the way the sunlight played on Chuck's tress-
es made the Fay Wray likeness all too real.

Kong 'came to life' and reared up. He grabbed
up ChuckFay in his mighty paw, as Jane and the kids
screamed *"Noooo!"* in unison. They drew their weapons and aimed.

But they held their fire. Not for fear of strik-
ing their dad. (They were better shots than that.)
They had no idea what the ape might do to Chuck if
they were to keep shooting.

Jane accepted the harsh fact that she may
never see her husband alive again. Maybe being part
of history wasn't such a great idea after all.

"He'll be alright, kids," she said in the kind of cheerful voice an insane person might use.

In the chaos and confusion, the llamas had freaked out and bolted away with the carts. The zombies got out of their way, tout suite. They sure didn't like llamas, those zombies.

* * *

Without the llamas to keep them at bay, the zombies began to crowd around the forklift. As they began to rock it back and forth, Jane was getting very claustrophobic, very quickly.

She reached down into the cab and lifted up the improvised weapon that she'd hacked together earlier—a pony methane flame-thrower made from one of the pressurized pony methane tanks.

Jane pulled the Zippo from her pocket and gave it a flick. As she turned the knob on the tank, there was a sudden...*FWOOOOMMMM!!!* A bright flame blasted out 30 feet.

Zombies lit up like yule logs.

Jane pivoted 360 degrees, creating a flaming zombie inferno 60 feet in diameter.

"Burn, zombies, burn!!!"

Dramatic, it was.

Clever, maybe not so much.

The family found themselves instantly surrounded by a sea of zombies flambé. The heat was intense. The children screamed as they fired full auto into the zombie inferno. The burning zombies continued to rock their perch. Roaring flames, fueled by desicated zombie flesh, came dangerously close to the Hesson's human flesh.

Realizing her miscalculation, Jane reached back into the cab and grabbed the fire extinguisher. She began spraying it into the faces of the zombies below, but quickly realized the futility of that.

A different course of action would be needed, and quick.

* * *

Kong ran towards the tower and leapt. He caught himself on the third floor and began climbing. The massive zombie beast had already set his jungle bride gently upon his shoulder, leaving Chuck to hold onto the monkey's thick fur for dear life.

Kong looked into the windows of the skyscraper. The first five stories were completely brimming with the undead. He could see nothing but undulating, blood-soaked zombies pressed up against the glass windows.

But as he passed the sixth and seventh floors, he could see terrified federal workers battling with brain-hungry zombies, who were pouring in through the stairways and elevator shafts.

It looked like zombies were even falling out of the duct work. New Detroit was in a full-blown panic.

* * *

Jane yelled at the kids to stop shooting and "hit the deck!"

They pressed themselves flat against the roof. The flames were licking over their heads.

Jane reached into her satchel and pulled out a hand grenade. She laid down on top of the children and pulled the pin, tossing the grenade into the crowd of flaming zombies standing directly in the way of the forklift.

KAAABOOOOOOOOMMMMM!!!!

The shockwave almost knocked Jane and the kids off the roof. The explosion blew up a whole bunch of zombies, sending many others reeling backwards—creating one of those domino effect clusterfucks that large groups of zombies sometimes found themselves trapped in.

The domino effect somehow blew out the fire directly in front of the fork lift. A path had been cleared.

Luckily, the machine was still idling...but was dangerously low on fuel. And it was looking like it might not be so easy to change tanks under the present circumstances.

Jane hung down, reaching into the driver's cage, and shifted the forklift into gear. She knew they only had a few hundred feet to get to the Windsor River. Of course, they'd be in the Windsor River swimming for their lives.

But at this point, it seemed like a no-brainer compared to remaining in Hart Plaza.

"Come on, kids!" Jane yelled. "We're getting the hell out of here!"

From their lying down positions, the twins continued spraying short bursts of suppression fire into the zombie throng. Jane continued spraying flames over the swarming zombie masses, to the sides and to the rear.

They slowly made their way across the crowded plaza, only making it about 35 feet before the path began to congest again with zombies.

* * *

Chuck looked up at the giant ape's ear. Holy shit, it was huge.

He wondered if he could climb up to it. Chuck pictured himself hanging on the ear with one hand, and a foot on the edge of the ear canal. He could see himself sticking his gun into the monkey's ear canal and killing its brain. He was pretty sure that'd be a good way to kill this monster.

He was also pretty sure there was no way in hell he could actually climb up to the ear to do that.

It was pretty much all he could do just to hang on tight right where he was. It was also quite probable that anything hanging off of someone's ear—be it human or giant ape zombie—would get slapped off pretty quickly.

Chuck was pretty sure that he would die if he tried to pull off such an action hero move.

First of all, the monkey would fall. Then what? He'd ride it down and try to jump off at the last second? Was that a real thing—or was that physics he'd learned from too many cartoons?

At that moment, Chuck honestly did not know the answer.

He thought for a moment that maybe he could throw a hand grenade in the giant's ear. That was also extremely unlikely and presented the same problem. He needed both hands to keep from falling off Kong. This damn monkey was moving all over. Heaving like a hairy, stinky ocean.

Chuck studied the window washing track that Kong was using as hand and foot holds. His brain had a notion that he might be able to jump off and hang on, then climb up...or down...or...

"No fucking way," he finally muttered to himself. "Just hang on for the ride."

*   *   *

"Get down!!!" Jane shouted as she tossed another grenade to clear the way.

The twins buried their faces in their arms.

BOOM!!

The path was cleared once again.

The steam engine forklift continued to propel them towards the water—and maybe even safety. The machine ran surprisingly well while running over so many corpses.

Jane and the kids could see the river ahead as they approached the edge of the plaza. As more and more zombies filled the plaza from beyond the city limits, the zombs who were already there had to go somewhere. Which led to a constant wave of zombies being pushed over the edge, where they fell into the river like lemmings.

If there's one thing that zombies are definitely not, it's swimmers.

There were hundreds of zombies floating face down in the river. As they approached the river of zombie corpses, Jane was now thinking that maybe this wasn't the greatest of ideas.

But at this point, there were no other ideas.

* * *

Chuck tried to look down to see if he could spot Jane and the twins. But he couldn't twist his neck around enough. All he could see was monkey shoulder and backside. With all that monkey motion going on, he began to get a little vertigo trying to look down.

He took a deep breath, looked straight ahead and focused on where he was—on the shoulder of a giant fucking ape!

"What the fuck?!" he thought. His day had started so normally.

He looked in some of the office tower windows and could see that desk jockey worker bees had barricaded all the office furniture against the doors and elevators.

"Good luck, guys," he thought.

* * *

The forklift came to a sudden stop, almost throwing Jane and twins into the drink. It had come up against a curb that prevented their pony buggies from rolling over the edge.

They could pretty much jump into the water from where they were. But the ever-swelling number of zombies floating gently down the stream made that very unappealing.

Plus, if they were to jump in the water with all their armament, they would surely sink and drown.

And not having that armament didn't seem safe at all. What about using a zombie as a flotation device? Would that even work?

Their attention was soon diverted as they took some time to stare at the vast sea of zombies coming their way through Hart Plaza. A constant flow of zombs flowing around them and into the Windsor River. It seemed endless.

They gazed across the plaza to the tower and looked up. They could see the giant ape making its way up the outside of the tower.

Did it still have Chuck!?

Jane and the twins could see that the ape did, in fact, have him in its paw when they last saw Chuck. But now, even at this distance, they could see that Zombie Kong was using both hands to climb.

"Maybe the ape put Chuck down somewhere safe," Jane thought to herself.

Unlikely as that was, the comfort she felt at just floating that trial thought balloon was a sentiment she thought worth sharing with the kids. "Maybe Daddy got put down somewhere safe." (Although, in this apocalyptic scenario she couldn't even imagine *any* place being safe.)

But the twins were only too happy to buy into it—the other possibilities being too unimaginable to even think about.

* * *

Chuck lost count of how many floors they had climbed. Looking straight up, it was hard to tell how many floors until the top. It was all so dizzying.

So he suddenly readjusted his gaze straight ahead.

Up, up, up they climbed, man and zombie monkey. 20 stories...30 stories...and then a noticeable wind picked up.

Chuck thought he saw something fly by, then something else. Then *another* thing. Whatever they were, they were big, with giant wings.

Chuck then realized he was surrounded by hundreds of flying creatures—six-foot monkeys... *with wings!* They wore ornate red bellhop vests, with shiny brass buttons, gold braids and fezzes.

Fezzes!

And they were carrying giant toothbrushes.

"What the fuck!?!" he yelled to himself in disbelief. "Okay, Chuck. Wake up! Any time now."

For a moment there, he was sure it was all a dream. The cognitive dissonance of the moment was a little too much. He was briefly convinced he should let go of Kong and sail gently to the ground.

Better yet, he would discover he could fly.

*   *   *

The flying winged monkeys had regrouped and now were swarming Kong from every direction. They were swooping in and poking at his head with their electric toothbrush cattle prods.

"Oh, great," thought Chuck out loud.

Kong took a swat with his mighty paw and knocked several of the mutants out of the sky. Their wings broken, the flying monkeys were sent into a downward spiral. Kong had his eye on one in particular, following it intently with his eyes and head.

When the monkey got too close, Kong lashed out. He snatched the creature, stuffing it into his mouth. The flying winged monkey screamed.

"Holy shit," Chuck muttered to himself.

He felt sick.

chapter 15

The rest of the family was finding their options rapidly dwindling.

When they were in the middle of the plaza, zombies were pushing the forklift from all sides. But now that they were on the edge of the plaza, the flaming zombies were flowing in only one direction—into the river.

The river was full of floating flaming zombies.

There soon became a mighty clot of zombs behind Jane and the twins that began to inadvertently shove their steam-powered forklift towards the river.

The front wheels were tight against the high curb. The rear wheels began to lift. Their perch began to shift.

"Hang on!!!"

"Ditch your long guns!"

"Nooooo!"

"Hold on tight!"

"Hit the deck! Fire in the hole!"

Jane pulled the pin from her last hand grenade and threw it in the middle of the zombie mob that was pushing on their forklift.

KABOOM!!!

The blast broke the logjam. The forklift's rear wheels hit the ground. Jane breathed a sigh of relief. But the effect was only temporary.

Before they knew it, several hundred more zombies were pushing against the forklift. The rear wheels lifted again. Their whole world was shifting.

Jane started screaming.

Undaunted, the flying winged monkeys continued their relentless attack on the great ape.

"Come on, ugly!" they taunted Kong. "We'll teach you to fly! Where are your wings?"

"Fly, monkey, fly!"

"Jump! Jump!"

"Hey! Fuck off!" yelled Chuck. One of the flying winged monkeys heard Chuck and promptly flew up to him.

"Hey! What are you doing here?"

"Never mind that!" Chuck screamed. "Please help me!!!"

"Okay," the flying winged monkey responded, as it flew towards Chuck for the rescue mission.

Kong could feel the beating wings in his ear.

He glanced back and, in an instant, snatched the creature from the air and stuffed it into his mouth. The flying winged monkey let out a terrible dying scream.

The rest of the flying winged monkeys backed off, out of Kong's reach, before quickly regrouping. After a midair huddle, the flying winged monkeys seemed to agree upon a new strategy. They pointed towards their crotches and then the big ape. They chose to target what surely must be his weak spot.

They began to focus all their efforts on using their shock-producing toothwands on Kong's massive hanging testicles. Even a giant zombie ape does not approve of having his testicles repeatedly shocked.

Kong contorted himself, trying to protect his exposed balls with his feet—while hanging on to the tower, more than 50 stories high.

* * *

Kong was going berserk. The flying winged monkeys stayed strategically out of reach and taunted Kong. He lashed out in vain. All the while, a stealthy and steady parade of flying winged monkeys continued to fly directly up the face of the building from underneath, tagging Kong's still exposed testicles with their magic electric shocking wands.

ZAP!!! ZAP!!! ZAP!!!

It felt like he was tea-bagging a hornet's nest. Kong was in no position to effectively deal with the situation.

Chuck was convinced he was going to die. He

wanted to shoot those motherfucking flying winged monkeys out of the sky. They were going to get him killed. They should be the ones dying, not him.

"What the fuck are you trying to do?" Chuck yelled into the wind. "He's a fucking zombie! If he falls down, he will just get up and climb again! Why do you care if he climbs this tower?!"

* * *

The raging zombie wildfire that Jane had started with the liberal use of her pony methane flamethrower had spread. Flames now raced across Hart Plaza, through the gates that led to the courtyard of the fortress Capitol Tower Complex.

The zombies on fire (not the band) continued their push towards the government compound. Flaming zombies (again, not the band) entered the atrium lobby of the Capitol Tower itself—the very tower that contained the last vestiges of the United States federal government.

The burning undead crawled on top of a squirming ocean of the undead, 10 zombies deep, spreading their wildfire like some sort of zombie virus. Soon, the fire, using the zombies as fuel, began to spread up the building's staircases. Terrible smelling smoke began to reach the upper floors. Fire alarms sounded. Sprinkler systems activated.

A happy-sounding voice intoned:

"Everything is under control.
Please do not panic.

Remain at your workstations."

In the meantime, the twins did the only thing they could do—they opened fire once again on the zombies.

Kong now tried a different tack for escaping the nonstop testicle shocks. He began pounding on the windows of the tower with his hands and feet. He smashed his fist through a window. With his improved grip, Kong was able to get some real muscle going and leveraged it into his smashing and destruction.

He soon had created an opening big enough to jump through. With Chuck still holding on for dear life, Kong swung his massive body up and through the gaping hole.

* * *

The High Council of Internet Memes had begun its emergency session hours earlier when news of the zombie uprising first came across the telegraph wires. After the roll call and the Pledge of Dental Allegiance, the council was apprised of the situation and immediately declared a state of emergency.

Technically, there had been an ongoing state of emergency declared for the past 50 years. When this was pointed out, they upped the ante and declared a Super Duper State of Emergency.

The High Council of Internet Memes had long ago become a fiasco of a ruling body, with terribly ill-defined rules of order. Its insistence on using the Occupy Wall Street method of 'mic check'—i.e., repeating everything that was said by any meme at any time—became an annoying and confusing method of communicating ideas.

Because there were no political parties, per se, it was every meme for themselves.

None of the splinter groups had enough votes. Everyone had their own agenda. Government hadn't functioned in decades.

Luckily, the Remaining United States of Upper America barely needed a federal government. Most interactions between the remaining states functioned just fine, actually. In reality, most of the states had been effectively running as their own nation states for quite some time.

The R.U.S.U.A. government's power barely reached past 8 Mile Road.

Soon, the High Council of Internet Memes would be the only thing standing between the superbrain-powered computer and a ravenous swarm of zombies.

* * *

All attention in the chamber was immediately drawn upwards. The High Council of Internet Memes looked up as an explosion of glass and giant monkey erupted above their heads.

Kong was followed into the hall by hundreds of flying winged monkeys, who flew in circles above the council chambers.

The 300 humans in the council chambers panicked en masse—shrieking, running for the exits, cowering under tables.

"Order! Order in the chamber!"

At the microphone, Jimmy McMillan III tried to maintain order.

"Order! Order in the chamber! Come to order at once!"

Kong landed flat on his back, crushing the entire cat meme delegation—Keyboard Kitty, Grumpy Cat, et. al. All killed. (Grumpy Cat had been an obstructionist. He wouldn't be missed.)

Kong rolled back and forth, cradling his balls and moaning.

"Get him!"

"Tie him up!"

"Council members! Help us hold the giant monkey down!"

There was nothing in the council chambers that could readily be used to tie down a giant monkey—except maybe all that velvet rope partitioning just above everything.

"Everyone! Grab some velvet rope and tie down the great beast!"

Dozens of brave memes grabbed as many lengths of the velvet rope as they could carry and ran towards the great ape. Flying winged monkeys swooped down and grabbed up as much velvet rope as they could fly with. Groups of memes tossed lengths of velvet rope over the rocking monkey to other groups of memes.

Flying winged monkeys wrapped coils of velvet rope around Kong's feet. The only thing impeding their progress was a simple lack of anything that might be used to lash the beast down.

"There you go, memes!"
"Don't give up!"
"You've got 'im now!"

* * *

Chuck found himself almost directly above Kong, on a crossbeam. The giant zombie ape had been immobilized on its back, arms pulled down to his crotch. A few dozen velvet ropes—along with the combined weight of 20 stout memes on each end—were able to hold him down. The flying winged monkeys had some luck, nearly hogtying Kong's feet, hands and balls together.

Chuck wanted to go for the kill. He removed a hand grenade from his satchel. He didn't want that sucker to bounce.

Chuck tore some drapery and loosely wrapped a bundle around the grenade. He felt confident that he could drop the explosive pillow on Kong's chest. Chuck's goal was to land it close to his throat.

With a little luck, he could explode its head off.

Chuck pulled the pin and tossed the package down between Kong's hunched shoulders. He was betting Kong's hunched shoulders would deflect the blast upwards, over the heads of the memes manning the ropes. It was a risk he was willing to take. In fact, he had taken it.

But the package being tossed caught Kong's eye. He looked up and saw Chuck. Their eyes locked.

Chuck held on as tightly as he could, anticipating the coming shock wave. He wrapped himself around the beam. Three...two...one...

KABLOOOOOOMMMM!!!

Chunks of hairy zombie monkey meat and bone showered down on the memes. The explosion knocked a dozen flying winged monkeys out of the air and bowled over the stout memes holding the ropes that held down Kong.

A terrible, terrible smell filled the chambers.

Chuck looked down as the smoke cleared. He could see a gaping chest wound, exposing jagged ribs and various viscera. He could also see Kong's face, contorted in rage.

Chuck's ears were ringing from the explosion. He couldn't even hear the monster's screams echoing throughout the chamber.

* * *

The forklift situation had reached a tipping point.

The twins had run out of ammo, just as Jane finished a hack that would turn her flamethrower methane tank into an exploding methane tank. She threw it as far as she possibly could.

But it wasn't quite far enough.

First nothing.

Then...

WABOOOMMMM!!!

The explosion blew the three of them off the roof of the forklift, now bound for the river. When it dropped into the water, the forklift sank—dragging several zombies with it.

Underwater, Jane looked all around for the twins. Then she looked up and realized she was floating up towards the open, flailing arms of a facedown zombie. These loathsome beasts looked even more horrific underwater.

Holding her breath, Jane kicked herself even deeper. Then...

FLABOOOOOOM!!!

The forklift steam boiler blew up underwater. A huge steam bubble rolled right by Jane and up to the surface, blowing zombies high into the sky. She saw her chance and swam furiously to a patch of open water that was suddenly free of flames and zombies.

Jane looked all around for the twins. But all she could see were burning, snarling, gurgling corpses floating in her direction.

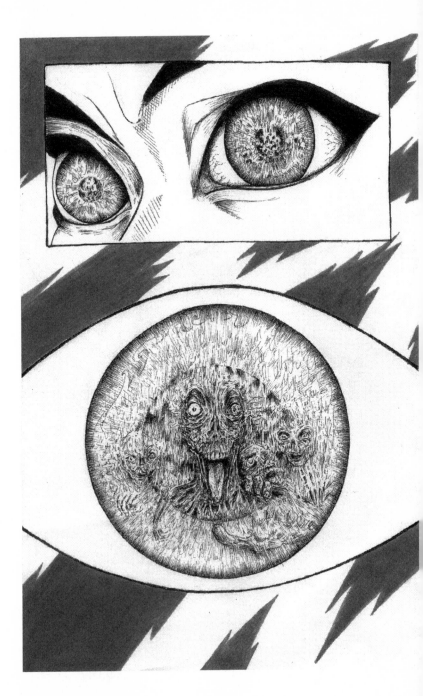

chapter 16

Zombie Kong rolled onto his side, struggling to get up.

He roared at the bravest of the memes, who were all looking for another in hopes of tying Kong down.

Then he managed to stand upright. Kong took a step, not realizing his feet were tied together, and fell flat on his face. His faceplant killed several council members.

Kong reached down and untied the knots, freeing up his feet. He stood up and ran towards the solid gold statue of Emperor Vermin Supreme across the chamber and gave it a bear hug before wrestling it off its pedestal.

He swung the statue around, smashing everything—all the windows, knocking down beams, knocking down the balcony. He was getting quite good at this smashing-shit-up-with-a-statue thing.

Remembering the unexpected surprises that were hidden above his head in the lobby, Kong swung for the ceiling. The statue's gold boot hat kicked its way through the floor above. Hundreds of brains in jars came tumbling down. Flying winged monkeys swooped down and caught as many as they could.

Alarms went off.

The computerized announcements became non-stop.

"Situation untenable."

"Brain breach has occurred."

"Lower floors no longer responsive."

"Flesh-eating zombies have broken security protocol."

"Building 7 has collapsed."

"Building 400 no longer responding."

"The building remains in lockdown. Please remain at your workstations. Everything is under control. Stand by for further updates. Have a nice day."

* * *

Kong jumped up to the overhead beam, where Chuck was inching his way towards the wall. The massive simian zombie swung back and forth a few times before pulling himself up. Standing on the beam, he was able to reach the jagged hole in the ceiling he'd created.

Kong stuck his head up through the hole and liked what he saw. He reached his arm in and scooped up hundreds of brain jars. He filled his maw and crunched away on the jars and brains.

Crunchy on the outside—soft and yummy on the inside.

Momentarily sated, he ducked out of the hole and walked along the beam with the grace of a circus monkey, on a direct path towards a terrified Chuck. Once again, he scooped Chuck up in his mighty paw.

"Noooooooooooo!!!" Chuck screamed.

* * *

"Mom! We're up here. Help us!"

Treading water, Jane looked up and saw her struggling children being held by hideous monsters—flying winged monkeys dressed like bellhops. She blinked in disbelief.

Then Jane felt herself being grabbed by the arms and shoulders. Thinking it was one of the flaming water zombies, she screamed. But when she realized that she was actually being carried off into the air by flying monkeys, she wailed again.

"Let me down!" Jane yelled.

"Okay," shrugged the agreeable monkeys, loosening their grip.

"No, don't drop me!" Jane shot back.

"Make up your mind," muttered one of the

monkeys.

Jane looked down at the zombie inferno. "Get us out of here," she told the monkeys.

As they beat their mighty wings, Jane fainted and went limp.

* * *

"Order! Order in the chamber! Come to order at once!"

The council tried to reconvene. Their optimistic streak served them 'til the bitter end. The council was fully aware of the zombies coming their way, inch by inch, floor by floor. But they seriously believed that the zombies would be stopped before reaching the council chambers.

Boy, were they wrong.

Zombies began pouring into the viewing gallery. The bravest memes fought for their lives. The cowards cowered and ran for the doors, where they were met by stairwells full of hungry zombies.

At the microphone, Jimmy McMillan III tried to maintain order. "Order. Order in the chamber! Come to order!!!"

This brave new experiment in democratic digital representation would soon come to a frightening end.

Soon, dude, there would be no quorum.

* * *

In the meantime, Kong had exited the council chamber through the hole he'd created. He continued to climb up the outside of the tower and its remaining 23 stories. Zombie Kong was climbing as fast as he could.

And Chuck was feeling pretty wrung out. His ears were still ringing. He was still in disbelief. He had no choice but to hold on tight for the ride.

Then Chuck looked up briefly. His eyes widened as he saw a large flaming object bearing down on him from above. He recognized it as some sort of motorcar from the olden times.

It was, in fact, a 2036 Dodge Pony, the last model year of the mass-produced gasoline-powered vehicle. During special monkey holidays, the simians made a sport of racing these relics around their makeshift track. They drove them fast and tantalizingly close to the outer edge of the skyscraper's roof. Occasionally one would go flying off into space. The driver would almost always get out.

Chuck had only seen such motormobiles in various history memes. He never dreamed he'd see one in person. And he most certainly would never have imagined he'd see one falling towards him from above, on fire no less.

Zombie Kong, who was focused on his climbing, didn't see the falling car. It smash-landed square on top of his head and bounced off. *Wham!* Chuck could feel the impact of the compact car. Stunned momentarily and seeing stars, Kong hugged tightly to the building as Chuck hugged tightly to Kong.

Chuck screamed as he saw another burning 2036 Jeep Pony barreling towards them from above.

Luckily, the vehicle's four wheels landed just right. The car glanced off Kong's shoulder and rolled right down his back, continuing on its gravity-fueled trajectory towards the street below.

Kong looked up and saw yet a third fiery car being pushed over the building's edge and falling towards him. But he was ready for it this time and easily deflected the flaming vehicle.

The flying chunks of charbroiled traffic seemed to stop as Kong shook his mighty fist skyward. Then the monster resumed his mission—climbing, climbing, climbing.

* * *

Kong reached the top of the boot tower and pulled himself onto the roof/sole. As he did, Chuck saw his chance. Suddenly and seamlessly, he dove off Kong's shoulder and onto the roof with a nifty tuck and roll.

The zombie ape didn't notice.

Kong pulled himself up the rest of the way and stood tall on top of the world. He beat what remained of his chest and roared, the wind whipping through his fur.

Zombie Kong declared his conquest over the city. He had won. He once again had dominion over all that he could see. The beast towered over the man he thought was his long lost love.

Kong had a huge erection.

Chuck looked up at the giant monkey silhouetted against the sky. He couldn't help but stare at the giant erection. He'd never been so far from the Earth.

Chuck had never been so scared.

Zombie Kong and his massive erection blotted out the sun. Then, out of nowhere, three hellfire sidewinder ponydrones ripped through Kong's mid-section, effectively cutting him in half.

The top half—his chest, arms, head and shoulders—toppled over the edge of the building, freefalling 73 stories. While his legs stood there momentarily—like Kid Sampson's in *Catch-22*—before falling over the edge and down into the street.

* * *

Chuck squinted into the sun, unsure of what he'd just seen. He didn't realize that he was now surrounded by flying winged monkeys. And he was being greeted with applause.

"Chuck!"

"Daddy!"

Chuck looked up to see his wife and children.

"Thank god, you're alive!"

His mind was officially blown. He and his family were now on the edge of a bustling, ramshackle, four-story shantytown on top of the world! So this was where the flying winged monkeys lived.

Monkey Town!

Jane led him down the alley into an interior courtyard, while Canadian prisoners of war—in their traditional red jumpsuits—shoveled monkey poop from the streets.

"Dear, this is Gen. Fred J. Muggs," Jane said

by way of introduction.

"How do you do, sir?" said Gen. Muggs.

He led the family down a series of alleys, to the president-in-exile's presidential shack. The flying winged monkey Muggs entered a darkened shack. The room was empty—but for a large video monitor and a small refrigerator on a platform.

He approached the fridge. In the door was a porthole. Through the small window stared a set of human eyes.

As Gen. Muggs opened the door, condensation spilled out. He removed the mysterious contents and carefully set the human head in its bubble jar, putting its base on top of the fridge.

* * *

"Your Excellency," Chuck said, respectfully addressing the head.

"Sooooo cold," said the head. "I've been watching a terrible zombie movie."

"Sir?"

"Yes, the zombies somehow escaped their bonds and amassed on the Capitol. They broke through the gates and lobbies, destroyed the gift shop and ate the entire High Council of Internet Memes. I've been watching them destroy row after row, floor after floor, of brains and more brains, for what seems like hours. Terribly implausible, but spellbinding nonetheless."

"Sir."

"Yes?"

"That was no movie you were watching."

"I see."

"Those are your brains."

"Oh..."

The upside down, rotted leather, galosh—with its blinking hi-tech gizmos and rusted buckles—had certainly seen better days. It was hard to tell where the boot ended and the head began. Needless to say, the 'living' head had also seen far better days.

"Sir! Do you not remember? It was all your idea, your master plan."

"Yessssssssssss...Of course...I remember now. In that freezer, my mind, it wanders. My phantom body, it aches all over."

"The plan is almost over."

"The plan is almost over?"

"Almost, your majesty. Just one more thing—we need the codes."

"It's for the best? You're sure?"

"Your idea has worked exactly as you had planned it—masterfully."

"Yes, everything according to plan. The important thing is that no ponies were hurt."

"Errr...Yes, your majesty. Ponies..." He uncomfortably looked away.

"We need the code to finish the project."

"Yes...the code...I knew the code yesterday... hmmm, let's seeee..."

171

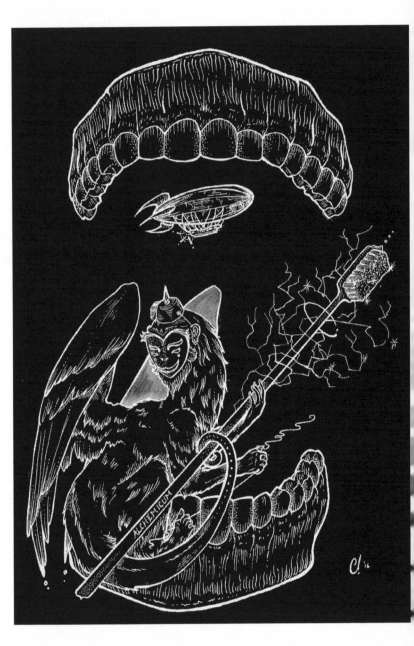

chapter 17

His once majestic beard was matted and gnarly—though his propensity for pronouncements remained unchanged.

"Bring me Dr. Zakk Von Flash."

"Yes, your excellency."

Gen. Muggs pulled the string that ran to the lab and rang the bell. Through two tin cans connected by taut wire, the order was placed.

"Bring me Dr. Von Flash."

"Yes, sir."

Thus summoned, monkey guards escorted Dr. Von Flash from his lab to the imperial head's storage shed. The guards gave him a little shove into the room. Once inside, he saw a number of familiar faces.

"Grandpa!"

"Chuck."

"Mr. Von Flash!"

"Jane."

"Great-Grampy Zakk!!!"

"Asher Lee. Charon. What on Earth are you all

doing here?"

"How did *you* get here?"

Who knew an impromptu Von Flash family reunion was in the offing?

"Silence!" demanded the head. "Mr. Von Flash! Where are we at with the project?"

The severed head was all business.

"I have done as you have asked of me," Dr. Von Flash said, hoping for some leniency and understanding. "I have undone my entire life's work. I have undone your entire life's work. Every zombie from within a 100-mile radius is now here in the Capitol. The very building upon which we stand is ready to burst at the seams, overflowing with the zombs. The massive combined weight of so many zombies is exceeding all the maximum load limits. The building itself could come down at any moment.

"The High Council of Internet Memes, which was your brainchild, has been devoured. As we speak, thousands of zombs are eating the nation's only superbrain computer—one million of your very own cloned brains. The brains that contain the entire history of our pony-based society are now an all-you-can-eat buffet. Every piece of information on every citizen collected over the last hundred years has been lost.

"You've got your wishes, sir. You—and I— have destroyed that which we helped create. Very few people have a chance to change the course of history. Few in history have the chance to make their dream become a reality. Fewer still have a chance to blow it all up. I hope you're satisfied. We'll be reunited one day—in hell. Now, release me and my family."

"Very well, Dr. Von Flash. I am a man of my word. You have served me and your country well. The plan would not have worked without your expertise."

"Gen. Muggs, see Dr. Von Flash and his family to the airship."

"Yes, your excellency."

"And make sure they have an adequate head-start."

"Yes, your excellency."

"Thank you, sir. I'd shake your hand..." Dr. Von Flash's voice trailed off.

"Yes, don't remind me," Emperor Supreme responded coldly. "Being disembodied has been a terrible thing. Being disemboweled was no great shakes, either.

"I have drifted from years of dreaming to screaming. Being drawn and quartered by my own royal ponies was quite traumatic. I have re-lived and re-died that scene a thousand times. Then to have my head saved and put into storage—followed by years of no sensory input. I was driven to near madness. I have hallucinated for years at a time.

"But I've also had time to reflect and introspect—time to second-guess, to imagine. I've had time to understand the ramifications of my decisions. I've outlived everyone I ever knew. I miss my body. I miss my arms, my hands, my cock. I want to join my body in the grave. Why have I been cursed with such a tragic existence?"

He began to wax nostalgically.

"When I was alive the first time, life was grand. The future was so bright that I required welding goggles. The old times were ending. The pony times were just beginning.

"I had a strong and clear vision. Some called it a delusion. Delusion or not, people shared in this dream. Not only did they feed into it, they actively worked towards it.

"I was able to pull America back from the abyss. I was able to lead a nation into a new world. I was able to institute a meme-based government for, of and by the people. I was able to end the use of planet-killing fossil fuels. I was able to rebuild the American economy from a stinking heap of rubble into a pony-based powerhouse that is the envy of the world.

"If it weren't for bold, decisive leadership, we'd still be living under the tyranny of the old constitution."

Asher poked Charon. "It's him," he whispered to his sister.

"Say something," Charon whispered back.

"No, you say something," goaded Asher.

* * *

"You're the giant holo-head from school, Vermin Sssuppreeeeme!" Charon said, unable to contain her excitement.

"The president," added Ash.

"Why, yesssssss, child," creaked Vermin's Teflon vocal cords.

"We were just learning about the War on Narnia!" Charon confessed.

"Allow me to let you in on a little top secret, children. Come closer."

Vermin's face twisted into a wry smile as the children stepped forward.

"There is no Narnia."

The children's faces displayed confusion, then frowns of cognitive dissonance.

"Where is the rest of your body?" demanded Asher Lee.

"It's a long story that I was telling before you interrupted me!" snapped the president. "Great. Now I forgot where I was..."

"You're in Monkeytown, on top of the world," Gen. Muggs helpfully interjected. "In New Detroit, Michigan."

"I know where I am. I just don't remember where I was...in the story. Oh, well. Suffice to say, all my great plans have come to naught, and everything I worked for has turned to shit."

"You know, things aren't really that bad..." said Asher.

"Yeah, we like it," chimed in Charon. "Everything was great until those zombies came along and ate all the..."

"Silence!!! Remove these insolent children."

"We were just leaving anyway."

"Not until my final exposition!" ordered the head. "It has taken many years to devise such a glorious plan to bring down the tower. My extended confinement in that glorified college dorm freezer was not in vain. My daring rescue by the flying simians will go down in legend. The Canadian prisoners of war were pivotal in my escape. They have earned their freedom. As we speak, they are being returned to their homeland."

It had been several years since the Emperor's head had negotiated his escape from the custody of the Remaining United States of Upper America, into the hands of the flying winged monkey's Republic of Monkeytown.

* * *

The Canadian POWs had ideal motivation and opportunity to cooperate with the monkeys. They were the only ones who had access to both the severed frozen head and total access to Monkeytown. The Canadians staffed the restaurant, shoveled the monkey poop, polished the brain containers and pretty much any other undesirable task required above floor 50.

When the actual transfer of the cryogenic mini freezer was made—from the royal suite on floor 72 up to the new presidential shack on the building's roof—no one even noticed.

The Royal Monkey Guard escorted the Von Flashes up floor after floor of rickety makeshift stairs. The race of winged monkeys was not known for its construction skills. It stunk from years of monkey piss and monkey shit.

Luckily, the Canadians were good at staying on top of the mess. There was nary a turd to avoid.

Finally, they reached the uppermost deck.

There, as promised, was a shiny, if refurbished, zeppelin. Like a weather vane, the sky ship pointed in the direction the stiff wind would propel them once untethered. Under the paint job, the faint outline of "reLOVEution RON PAUL 2012" could be discerned.

One at a time, the Von Flash family gingerly climbed aboard and crawled up the visibly swaying structure leading to the gondola. It was something more than a ladder—but something less than stairs. It didn't help that there was no railing.

The five Von Flashes crowded into the small compartment. It was a wondrous place to be. Looking down, they could see hundreds of red clad POWs standing in line. The line curled around and ended near the edge of the tower, at the tip of the boot.

It appeared they were lining up to jump off.

After a second look, the truth became apparent—the Canadians were waiting for their turn at zip-lining. Zip lines had been surreptitiously strung up, running from the toe tip of the tower, across the Windsor River, and into the heavily domed city of Windsor.

One after the other, the Canadians took flight, straight back to Mother Canada.

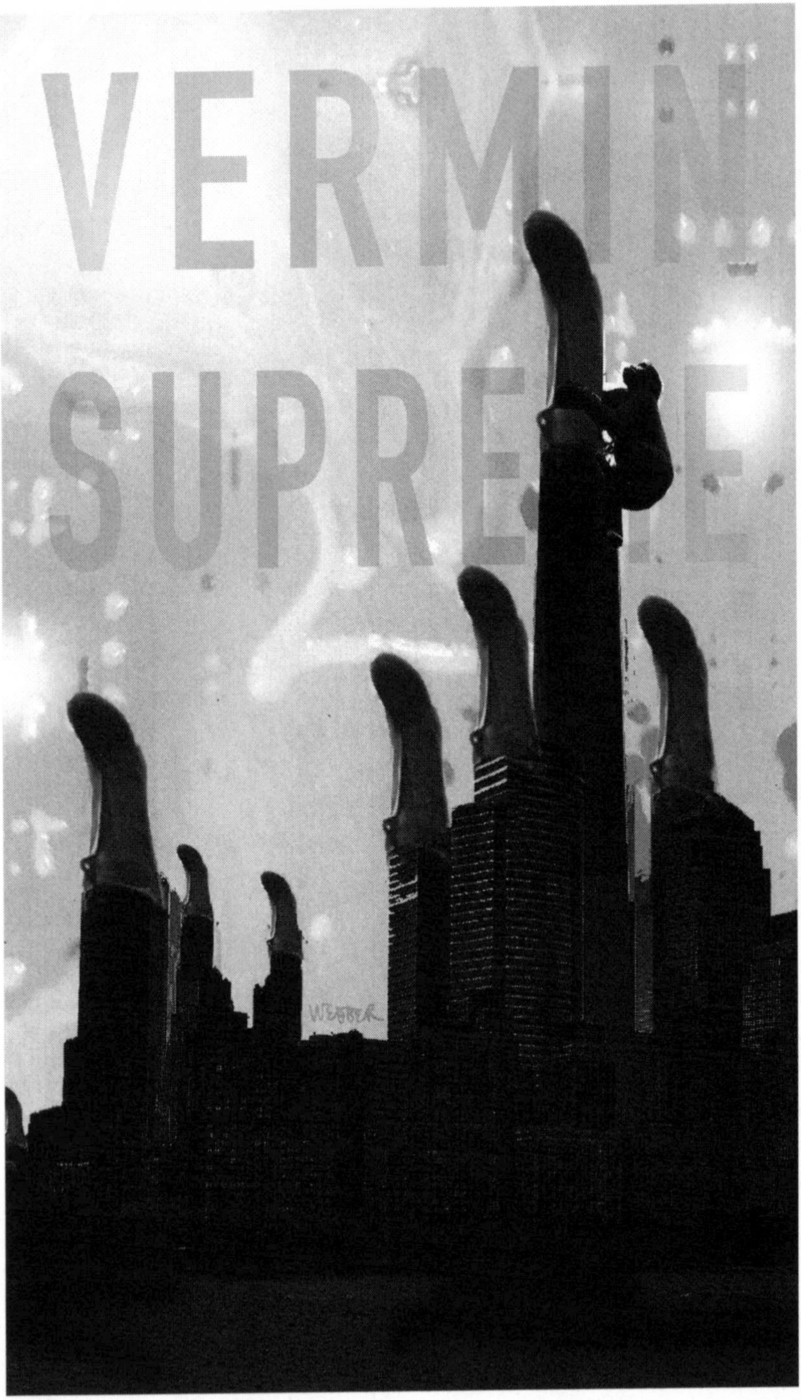
VERMIN
WEBBER

chapter 18

"Excuse me, kids," Dr. Zakk Von Flash said as he bellied up to the control stick. "I used to fly one of these in the war."

"The war against Narnia?" Charon asked hopefully.

"No, this was a real war. One they don't teach you about in school. It was the war between the Remaining United States of Uppper America and the United Westboro Baptist States of God Hates Fags America. Now that was a real war. Out of all the wars President Supreme started, this was probably the most justified. We zombie bombed the shit out of them. I was on the bombing run that dropped the supersized pony zombies into the Phelps' presidential palace. They never knew what hit 'em."

Gen. Muggs interrupted. "Dr. Von Flash, I wanted to thank you on behalf of my people."

"Sir, I have always been for the monkeys. I certainly didn't do it for that madman. You will see that he gets what's coming?"

"Of course," Gen. Muggs said, giving the signal to release the tether.

With a pop and a bob, the blimp lurched forward and into the airstream.

Meanwhile, Gen. Muggs returned to the presidential head shack.

"Sir, it is time. We need the codes."

"Very well. Ask me the security questions."

"What is your favorite color?"

"Blue..."

"...and?"

"That's it."

"What's it?"

"The code. That's it."

"Blue is the code?"

"Yes. Code blue. Get It?"

"Not much of a code..."

"You didn't guess it."

Gen. Muggs entered the code word. But entering the code was irrevocable. The final countdown was beginning. The last of the Canadians zipped across the river.

"Self-destruct sequence activated. Ten Minutes.
Please remain at your workstations.
Smile and have a nice day."

* * *

There was no one left alive inside the towers to hear the announcement. The entire population of Monkeytown took to the sky, en masse. They flapped their mighty wings as fast as they could in the direction of the blimp.

Below, the streets roiled with zombies.

"Goodbye, Emperor Supreme. Good Luck."

"Thank you, Gen. Muggs. Now go join your people."

The head that once ran the world watched the cloud of monkeys fly into the sunset, towards the rapidly receding blimp. The sun slowly set over the horizon. He could feel the warmth of the burning shantytown at his back—the back of his head, rather.

Sparks blew high over his headboot in the direction of the wind. The snaps and pops of the crackling fire filled his ears. He could smell the smoke. It was a beautiful sunset.

> *"Self-destruct sequence activated.*
> *Please remain at your workstations.*
> *Smile and have a nice day."*

"I have no regrets," he said to himself. Time slows when one is at peace.

> *"Five minutes..."*

Without warning, a circle of shimmering liquid fire appeared, hovering in the air directly in front of him. Charging at full speed, a gleaming, headless robopony leapt from the portal, skittering and clattering onto the ledge of the skyscraper.

It skidded to a halt.

Its rider—a younger version of the dapper,

boot-headed, full-bodied Vermin Supreme—dismounted with style and grace.

This Vermin, shiny and as yet unjaded, approached his own disgruntled, disembodied head from the future.

"Seriously?" the head muttered.

Youthful Vermin, his beard not yet white, was shocked and appalled at the poor condition of his head in the future.

"Holy crap! What have they done to you? To me?" He reached out to touch himself.

Answering the age-old parlor game question, "What would you say to your younger self?" the head responded sternly.

"I feel fine. Don't touch me. You're not me. You're a young and stupid kid. You'd better get out of here. This whole place is about to blow."

When his younger self wouldn't budge, the Vermin head got frustrated. "Why are you here?" he demanded.

"I'm here to rescue you!" said young Vermin gallantly.

"I don't want to be rescued!" screamed the Vermin head.

"What? C'mon..."

"Now git, you simpleton!"

"Two minutes. Self-destruct sequence activated.
Please remain at your workstations.
Smile and have a nice day."

"I'm not leaving without you."

The head wished desperately that it had been equipped with weaponry of some sort.

"Seriously?" he gnashed his teeth, trying to throw out a warning sign. "Don't make me bite you."

An empty threat, as he was essentially in a glass jar.

"Yoink!" said the full-bodied Vermin as he slipped around the table and grabbed the head unit from behind.

"Leave me alone!"

"Neverrrrrr!!!"

Young Vermin screwed the base of the head unit into the head socket of the robopony.

"Stop spinning me! You're making me dizzy."

The screwing finally stopped when the head unit clicked into place. The interface worked immediately. The head immediately felt its awesome new robopony body.

"Whoa, Nelly!"

* * *

The robopony body was immediately ready to carry out the will of its new brain. Hydraulic fluid coursed through his new veins. Pistons pumped furiously. The head had been weaponized.

Vermin the younger mounted his stainless steel steed, strapping in.

"One minute..."

The Vermin-headed cyborg robopony roared

to life. It reared up and danced on its two rear legs. The head laughed maniacally and fired his new bad-ass twin Gatling guns into the sky. Ratatatatatatattatatat!!!

"30 seconds..."

"Bwa hahaha. Fuck you, sonny. I'm taking you with me!"

Robopony Vermin ran full speed around the racetrack, around the edge of the tower, firing his machine guns and launching hand grenades into the abandoned shantytown.

"Kaboom!!!" Robopony Vermin squealed in glee. "WooHooo!!!"

"Five..."

Vermin held on tight to the bucking robot, trying to reach the manual overdrive switch. It was inconveniently located just out of his reach. He realized he should have waited until after the portal jump before making the interface.

"Live and learn," he thought.

"Four..."

"And now we die—bwahahahahaha," robopony Vermin said with a sinister laugh.

He leapt over the upper body of Kong—who had somehow reassembled himself and was climbing back up the tower. Oh, shit! Just as Kong was reaching the top of the tower, robopony Vermin jumped off the building, as far out into space as he could possibly leap.

As the two Vermin Supremes began their freefall, Kong swung out after them, diving in right behind them.

"Three..."

Young Vermin, clutching onto roboVermin's back, frantically fumbled for his keychain, clicking the button repeatedly with his thumb.

"Two..."

The no-frills emergency portal finally opened up directly below the falling duo.

"One..."

Without fanfare or warming, they disappeared into the darkness of the unknown.

* * *

Unlike the finely coordinated portal that brought Vermin Supreme here, the Emergency Portal offered no guarantees. A nanosecond after Kong fell through after them, the hole turned inside itself and disappeared.

Just then, the trigger ignited the nuclear explosion. The towers and the zombies were instantaneously incinerated—Hart Plaza nothing more than a pile of dust and debris.

The massive flock of flying winged monkeys had caught up to the zeppelin. A flash, brighter than the brightest lightning, lit up the sky.

"Wow."

Looking around for a very long moment, everyone appeared to be skeletons, as the x-ray energy tore right through them. A moment later, the sound followed. Then the shockwave.

The entire flock of flying winged monkeys was thrown tumbling. Somehow, they were all able to catch themselves before even coming close to hitting the ground.

The zeppelin pitched and bobbed. It spun around wildly before regaining control. Looking back, the monkeys could see the roiling mushroom cloud reaching up into the sky. The monkeys let loose with a collective shudder as they realized there was no going home.

Down in the cockpit, things were very quiet. Finally, Dr. Von Flash broke the silence.

"Why that old so and so," he said. "I should have known he had one more trick up his sleeve."

chapter 19

(epilogue #1)

"Goodnight, kids."

"Grandpa, tell us a story..."

"...about growing up in the old world."

As any grandpa is happy to tell a story, Asher Lee was all too happy to share his.

"Once upon a time, there was a period in history when people got around on great, monstrous, four-legged beasts. They were the largest mammals on the planet. They were animals called 'ponies.'"

"Poneez?"

"And all the electricity in the world was produced by creatures called 'zombies.'"

"Zombeeeezzz?"

"Eeelectriciteee?"

"There was a great city, with towers that reached into the sky! And a president named Vermin Supreme ruled the world."

"Supreeeeeeme?"

"Your great-great-grandpa knew the president, personally. Well, at least his head."

The children looked at each other, a little confused. Asher realized he was getting ahead of himself. No pun intended.

He told them of their old home, of his old school, of his sister and parents, of the checkpoints. He gave them a brief history lesson on the R.U.S.U.A. He wanted to tell them everything he could remember about that fateful day.

There was no need for embellishment.

* * *

After every phrase, the children would quizzically repeat one of the words. English was not their first language.

By the time Asher even got to the day of the Great Zombie Escape, the children were fast asleep.

The recollections of those times came back vividly to him.

He remembered the blimp ride. Sailing through the sky with his family.

He remembered the crash landing in the canopy of a great forest.

He remembered helping build a shelter from the zeppelin skin. Life without ponies was hard at first, but they quickly grew accustomed to their new lifestyle.

He remembered playing with all the little flying winged monkey children. He was the only human boy in the forest. It put him at a distinct disadvantage in many monkey games. All the monkey children admired the fact that it was his grandpa that nuked New Detroit, freeing them.

He remembered growing up and becoming a man. He remembered falling in love with a beautiful flying winged monkey girl. He remembered their many years of happiness together.

There was some concern in the village when the union resulted in a pregnancy. The monkey midwives paid close attention. Luckily, the children were born perfectly normal. Following their matrilineal line, they all had functioning wings.

Asher guessed he was thankful for the path of history. He'd experienced the end of the old world— and the birth of the new.

He'd seen zombies.

He'd ridden ponies.

He'd even met the president's head.

He supposed it was a bad thing that his own grandfather was kidnapped and forced to work for an insane head, destroying the American government and every last zombie and pony.

Dr. Von Flash's complicity in the destruction of New Detroit weighed heavily on the doctor. He resented being held captive and being forced to erase his life's work. He was not keen on causing such mass human terror. He had terrible nightmares.

After all, it was he who had secretly introduced the pony-eating behavior into the zombies. He hated ponies and had grown to hate the president's head. He knew how much it would hurt the dictator.

Dr. Von Flash learned to brew his own alcoholic beverage from the plentiful berries in the forest. Although he enjoyed the flying winged monkeys, a creature he'd helped create, the doctor had trouble adapting to his new life in the forest. He wasn't particularly fond of trees.

He eventually drank himself to death.

* * *

Asher Lee drummed up some warm thoughts about his great-grandfather. He stroked the children's downy wings and kissed their little furry foreheads.

He remembered, clearly, looking at that head in the glass bubble. Even magnified by the glass, it seemed shriveled.

Sometimes, he wondered what that head was thinking.

chapter 20
(epilogue #2)

"Dammit," the Vermin Supreme head was thinking. "Where the hell is this? Was the explosion a dud? What happened? Am I dead?"

They were somersaulting, ass over tea kettle.

They were spiraling in a barrel roll.

There was nothing but darkness.

There was no sound.

They certainly had trajectory and velocity. They were moving through space at a high rate of speed. There was no friction to slow them down. It wasn't clear whether they were subject to the effects of gravity.

Falling requires a context of up and down. In this blackness, it was impossible to tell.

"Not too shabby," the elder disembodied head of Vermin Supreme thought to himself in regards to his new re-embodiment. "I wonder if it comes in other versions." He wondered this while flexing his pistons.

Meanwhile, he continued to try and buck off his new nemesis.

"Was I ever that young?" he mused. He kicked wildly, arching and twisting his back as far as it would go.

He had destroyed New Detroit and its terrible bureaucracy. He had orchestrated it all. The zombies did his dirty work. They killed the entire federal government. They ate the finest minds of their generation. The High Council of Internet Memes was no more.

Then he, in turn, had killed all the zombies with an atomic bomb.

It was a perfect plan. He got his revenge.

He'd set the flying winged monkeys free. He'd released the Canadians. He ended the failed experiment of memeocracy. He'd go down in history as America's greatest president.

The terrible and collateral carnage to his beloved ponies was still unknown to him.

* * *

He fired his Gatling guns and lasers in all directions. Tracers and light beams peppered infinity, lighting up the darkness. For purposes of safety, they were designed to not accidently shoot the rider.

In this case, the design also prevented the ponybot from intentionally killing its passenger.

Vermin Supreme, younger and from some parallel dimension and perpendicular time, held on to the bucking, spinning, cyborg.

"Fucking cyborg pony!" Vermin muttered, his

rubber boot-hat bouncing and flopping crazily.

Oh, he knew he had screwed up. He never should have attached the headpiece onto the robo-body before the portal leap.

"There was no other way," he assured himself. It would have taken two arms just to hold the head unit. He needed both hands to control the mechanical equine and set the portal projector.

Who knew his head from the parallel future/past would be so resistant to being rescued?

He had one foot locked into the stirrup and one hand locked on the saddle horn. The embodied Vermin flailed as he tried to get back in the saddle. He knew that passing through a portal took only a second, to the casual observer, on either end.

Inside the wormhole, though—due to the relativity factor—it seemed like it took forever. Usually, the trip resembled a sensory depravation tank. Lots of time to relax and gather one's thoughts. It was a fairly pleasant way to travel.

Not this time, though. This life and death struggle was a far cry from the usual placid commute.

* * *

After a while of interminable tumbling, Vermin the Younger was able to get ahold of a reign and regain his mount. He leaned forward and wrapped his arms around the glass housing unit, trying to peer inside. The head inside rotated until it faced backwards.

The mechanical struggle ceased. The falling continued. The wrinkled, furrowed brow of the somewhat shrunken, wizened head furrowed a little more. For just a moment, he felt a tenderness for his younger self.

He wanted to look himself in the eye.

CyborgPonyVerminHead flicked on all his lights at once. Beams of brightness pierced the black night. He could see his younger face pressed up against the glass of his tank.

"Dammit, he's gonna get snot on my glass. I should've kept one of those Canadian squeegees," he said, using the derogatory term for Canadian POWs.

His moment of tenderness had passed.

The rear-mounted spotlights allowed Vermin the Head the increasingly frightening view of Zombie Kong—hot on their tail.

The monster's face was contorted by the G forces. His eyes were burning reflective coals. His fangs were fearsome. He swung his arms, alternating between a swimming motion, in an attempt to propel himself, and a grabbing motion.

RoboPonyVerminHead hoped he could slow down enough to allow the monster monkey to tear his younger self apart.

Maybe then he, himself, would also cease to exist. It was worth a try.

"Stupid Emergency Deployment Portals," thought young Vermin.

He questioned his decision to rescue his own disembodied head.

He hoped that it would be worth it.

He would find out soon.

THE END???

ABOUT THE AUTHOR

photo: Marc Nozell

VerminSupreme2016.com
WhoIsVerminSupreme.com
VerminSupremeStickers.com

"There were harsh political realities when President For Life Vermin the First took office. At the time of his ascent to the White House there were over 300 million Americans living within America's previous borders. At the time, there were only 200,000 ponies in the entire country. It was a recipe for civil unrest. Those were not just political realities, they were reality realities.

There was a very stark choice to make. Would it be the mass execution of some 299,800,000+ Americans in order to achieve proper pony/human parity... or something else? Although there were drawbacks to consider—mostly just questions of ethics and public relations—the population was demanding their ponies. Ponies that were nowhere in sight. It was a time of heightened international tensions. No one would have blamed Tyrant Supreme if he had ordered the National Dental Guard to carry out a full-scale massacre of the civilian population.

It was high time, actually.

The veneer of civility that had protected Americans from such real political unrest for quite some time was wearing thin. The quaint and oft repeated notion that, 'It can't happen here,' was truly just a lack of imagination. It didn't help at all that recently installed Dictator Forever Vermin Supreme was completely and utterly insane.

How this deranged hobo made it all the way into the White House was still not completely understood."

ARTISTS

JOHN HAGEN-BRENNER (Chapters 7 & 13) AKA: Hellswami Satellite Weavers. Charter Member—The Church of the SubGenius. Urban, Post-Industrial aboriginal. Hand-crafted world view. Oblique. Tangential. Loose cannon. Has no social filter. Plays well with others. When he speaks, says whatever is on his mind. Skews every thought along the most amusing trajectory, irrespective of his actual personal feelings about the subject. To see more of his work go to—

http://tinyurl.com/jko7hee
http://tinyurl.com/z9bzt6o
http://tinyurl.com/jcp6xnu

KIERA HAGEN-BRENNER (Chapter 4) is currently a full-time student studying animation and illustration at California State University, Northridge. A soon-to-be graduate, she is looking for employment opportunities in the field of animation. Kiera is also illustrating a comic that has yet to be published. She lives with her sister and parents near Los Angeles, CA. Her father, John Hagen-Brenner, also created art for this book. To see more of her work go to—

http://kierahb.wix.com/porfolio

ELENORE "ELLIOTT" ELENA (Chapters 14 & 16) was raised in Ridgewood, NY by loving parents, Judith & Nelson. Elenore goes by many names—lately Elliott has been a favorite. Elliott is an artist, musician and teaching-artist, specialized in leading school mural projects. They have created murals in public schools in NYC and abroad in Costa Rica, and aspire to travel the planet making more. Elliott's currently working on a feminist rage teenage werewolf graphic novel about violence, PTSD, sexual harassment/assault, solidarity and healing. You can see more of their work at—

humdrop.squarespace.com

MARGEAUX HUFFINES-KEENER (Chapters 3, 11 & 20) was born and raised in Richmond, VA, where art saved her from "everything that ever tried to destroy my spirit and vitality for life. I express with my hands the duality of human nature and perceptions of reality; our conflicting capacity for kindness and desires for darkness." Margeaux adds, "I will live forever through the art that sweats out from my pours, dirties my nails, musses wildly through my hair and runs coarsely through my veins." You can find her wherever there is art to be made. If you would like something made, she can be found at—

http://www.iammargeaux.com/contact

CIEL INCARNADINE—née Feliza Bruzzone in Bogotá, Columbia—(Chapter 17) is a trained mask maker, collage crafter, costume designer, traveling illustrator, non-gallery curator and semiotics aficionada. Born into a family of visual artists and alchemists, she's experimented with a wide range of media and exhibited her work in various cities along the Americas—from Barranquilla to New Orleans to Panamá to California to New York, where she now resides. When Ciel's not investing her time in various forms of human expression, she finds grounding in the natural sciences—both in the field and in the classrooms, having worked with the Smithsonian Tropical Research Institute and the American Museum of Natural History from 2008 to 2016. She's currently working on making her way back across the Atlantic Ocean to Europe to seek an apprenticeship in tattooing, the continuous search for sustainability and maybe cheaper rent. See more of her art at—

alchemicum.com

JEREMIAH LABIB (Chapter 12) has been drawing pretty much his entire life. Whether it be doodles on his homework or crude drawings on napkins, he always got a thrill out of illustration and creating something from his own imagination—usually monsters and creatures with absurdly elongated proportions and haunting ferocity. "This is something I wish to accomplish in my art: to let the viewer get lost in detail and, hell, have a bit of a laugh as well at the drawing's overall absurdity. I'm always going to be drawing, no matter where my life takes me. I'm always going to try and improve myself as an artist as well as a creator. Guess we'll see where it all goes." Explore more of his work at—

www.JeremiahLabib.wix.com/jwlillustrations

AARON MAKELA (Chapter 2) is an artist living in Los Angeles, CA. He met publisher, Bob Makela, when he was 9 years old and living at the Hollygrove orphanage in Hollywood. He's since done graphic art projects for various charities and is active in the Covenant House program to help troubled youths. You can learn more about his story here—

http://tinyurl.com/owsuhh8

TONY MILLIONAIRE (Chapter 1) is the creator of *Maakies*, one of the most celebrated weekly comic strips in America, which has been a regular feature in the *Village Voice*, *LA Weekly* and the *Chicago Reader*, among many other publications. Look for Tony's new book, *Drinky Crow Drinks Again*, wherever books are sold. His work can be found at—

Maakies.com

RICHIE MONTGOMERY (Prologue) is a philosophical surrealist artist whose work is highly regarded for its unique twist on life and our perspective of it. The "hidden in plain sight" details of his work are remnants of the great masters like M.C. Escher and Salvador Dali. His work takes an extraordinary amount of time to complete and is sure to keep you asking questions forever. The more you look into his art, the more you will see. The details are quite mind blowing. His website is at—

ElectricKoolaidArt.com

NINA PALEY (Chapter 5) is the creator of the animated musical feature film *Sita Sings the Blues*. Her adventures in our broken copyright system led her to join QuestionCopyright.org as Artist-in-Residence in 2008, where she produced a series of animated shorts about intellectual freedom called *Minute Memes*. More recently she made *This Land Is Mine*, a short film about Israel/Palestine/Canaan/the Levant intended for a new feature film, *Seder-Masochism*. To see more of her work go to—

NinaPaley.com

DALE RAWLINGS (Chapter 8) is a cartoonist/illustrator living in the heart of darkness (the Washington, D.C. area) and is the byproduct of a genetic experiment gone awry. He is infamous for his comics work in *Skidoo*, *Down and Out On Planet Earth*, *District Comics* and *Magic Bullet*—and he is a member of the DC Conspiracy. He currently makes a satirical political webcomic called *Jesus 2016* that mostly updates weekly. His work can be seen at—

www.Jesus2016TheComic.blogspot.com
TheDuckWebComics.com
ComicFury.com

SETH TOBOCMAN (cover) is a neo-expressionist comic book artist who started drawing before he could read and hasn't stopped for long since. After introducing Harvey Pekar to cartoonist Gary Dumm—the duo who'd go on to create the iconic neo-realist comic book *American Splendor*—Tobocman eventually went on to become an outsider icon in the comic book world himself, inspired by the likes of William Burroughs, Pablo Picasso and David Bowie. His anti-war adult comic book, the alternative magazine *World War Three Illustrated*, found a worldwide audience and Tobocman has since published books

(*You Don't Have to Fuck People Over to Survive*, *War In the Neighborhood*), been involved in New York City politics, produced art on the Israel/Palastine conflict (the book *Portraits of Israelis and Palestinians*, the art show *Three Cities Against the Wall*) and taught comics at the School of Visual Arts in New York City. For more on his story and art go to—

SethTobocman.com

ROD WEBBER (Chapters 9, 15, 18-19) is an artist, author, musician and filmmaker. He has directed ten feature films, released 20 CDs and was a regular on the college radio charts when there was such a thing. He was the former co-host of the Swasey Show on WFNX in Boston and is a regular contributor to DailyKOS. His books include *The Garden of Voiceless Screams* (a collection of paintings) and *Poetry of the Malfunctioning Engine* (a text-to-voice novel). His videos across YouTube and Vine have collectively amassed 17 million views and his films have starred celebrities from Stan Lee to Greta Gerwig to ambassadors and heads of state. His current documentary, tentatively titled *Fighting Evil with a Flower*, documents Webber's social experiment in which he traveled the U.S. giving flowers to strangers in the street, and how this transformed into praying onstage with the likes of Jeb Bush, John McCain and most of the other 2016 candidates. (Including Vermin Supreme.) Most recently, he put flowers in the barrels of AR-15s held by an open-carry group at a Donald Trump rally in Dallas, recreating the famous "Bernie Boston" photo. He is writing a new book about the experiment. For more on Rod go to—

RodWebber.com
http://shop.spreadshirt.com/rodwebber
wikipedia.org/wiki/Rod_Webber
www.imdb.com/name/nm2369219

ORANGE ZEPPELIN (Chapters 6 & 10) has been drawing ever since she was old enough to not try to eat crayons. Her passion for creating art has only gotten stronger over the years and she is usually working on anywhere from 3 to 345 different projects at any given time. Being very multi-craftual, she enjoys experimenting with a wide variety of media and styles, and is influenced by a wide variety of artists. In addition to fully supporting the candidacy of Vermin Supreme, Orange is a rabid metalhead and cactus hoarder. You can find more of her art on antisocial networking sites such as—

DeviantArt: orange-zeppelin.deviantart.com
Facebook: www.facebook.com/OrangeZeppelinArt
Tumblr: orangezeppelin.tumblr.com/

Also from **Bobtimystic Books**—

The Can't-idates: Running For President When Nobody Knows Your Name

(Featuring an entire chapter on Vermin Supreme!)

And many more...